SEDUCING YOU

TRACY BROEMMER

Seducing You

by

Tracy Broemmer

Contemporary Romance Novella

Published by Tracy Broemmer

Edited by Lexie Broemmer

Cover by Tracy Broemmer

ISBN: 978-1-951637-71-2

Names, characters, and incidents depicted in this book are products of the author's imagination or are used fictitiously. Any resemblance to actual events, or person, living or dead, is coincidental and not the intent of the author.

CHAPTER ONE

Chantele

“Dibs on the guy in the cowboy hat.”

“No kidding, Chan.” Nova Brathwaite rolled her eyes. “The bet *was* a cowboy.”

Chantele Morgan eyed the two guys bellied up to the bar. Both were dressed in jeans that displayed their assets nicely, both wore cowboy boots, but the guy on the right wore a worn-looking cowboy hat and the one on the left wore nothing on his dark hair.

“The other guy looks as much like a cowboy as the hat guy,” she decided. She pounded the rest of her longneck and looked around the bar.

“So?”

Chantele looked at her other friend and arched her eyebrows. “What?”

“What’s your plan?” Paisley Hathaway sipped from her club soda, put her glass down, and watched Chantele with a smirk. Chantele had thought marriage had made her friend Paisley glow, but the baby she was carrying—never mind that it was roughly the size of a plum—brought out a shine in Paisley’s eyes Chantele hadn’t seen in twenty-seven years of friendship.

“What?” Chantele relaxed back in her chair and waved a hand over the silky tank and skimpy bra that barely covered her own assets. “This isn’t enough?”

Across the table, Nova snorted. She finished her cocktail and looked around for their waitress. The Iron Stag was a mix of trendy and greasy spoon, and the result was bizarre, yet interesting. The three of them had come here mostly because it was the closest place to the VRBO house they’d rented for the weekend. There weren’t a lot of bars or restaurants near Rodey, Kentucky; if they wanted a change of scenery later or tomorrow, they would have to pile in Paisley’s SUV and head to Kissing Springs, Kentucky. The Bourbon Boot Scoot sounded like a fun bar. And they could always check out the male revue that performed at The Boyd Theater.

If Chantele struck out here with the cowboy at the bar.

Paisley grinned and shrugged. “Absolutely enough, but you gotta get him to turn his head this way before he sees ‘em.”

“True.” She looked around again. “I was thinking some line dancing.”

“Girl, you need a pole, not a line.” Nova shot her a frown.

Chantele dropped her head back for a full-throttle laugh. She felt her cheeks heat with the suggestion, but the lighting in the bar was good for hiding things like blushes.

"She can shake her ass with the best of them," Paisley reminded Nova, who pointed at her with her glass still in hand.

"Well, how's this for starters." Chantele stood and reached for Nova's empty highball glass.

"What're you doing?" Nova cut loose with a rip of her contagious laughter.

Chantele winked at Nova. "Since our waitress is working so hard, I'm gonna go to the bar and get us another round. Pais? You need another club soda?"

"Nope," Paisley answered with a sigh. "I'm driving."

Chantele laughed softly and nudged her shoulder. "You wanted that little bun in your oven."

"Six more months." Paisley's fake groan didn't fool Chantele.

"Longer if you breastfeed," Chantele reminded her. "Just sayin'."

"Not sure she wanted the bun in her oven," Nova mumbled, "but she sure as hell likes the sausage that put it there."

"Jesus." Chantele rolled her eyes. "I'll be back, *ladies*."

The jukebox—apparently, the Iron Stag was behind the times as far as DJs and music machines, but they did have a live band playing *next* weekend—played "Maybe It Was Memphis" as she made her way up to the bar. Her cheeks tingled a bit knowing her friends were watching her, expecting her to say something to the cowboy.

She would, but she wasn't sure this was the right time. First, she just had to catch his eye. Get him to notice her. She could do that. That part wasn't a problem. But Chantele wasn't much for hookups. Unfortunately, that was the crux of the bet. Her friends—she'd been besties with Paisley since kindergarten and Nova had wandered into the fray in junior high—knew she wasn't a hookup kind of girl and had bet her she couldn't ride a cowboy before the weekend was over.

Never mind that they were here for Paisley. To get Paisley out for one more good time before the baby she carried was bigger, before she was exhausted, and maybe even dealing with morning sickness. The three of them had always gone all-in with dares and bets. Chantele supposed she'd started it back in tenth grade when she dared Nova to offer the varsity quarterback a blowjob. When she'd reported back after the party they'd all crashed, Chantele and Paisley had believed her without question. They'd seen Nova sneak off with him, and they'd seen him appear by the bonfire about fifteen minutes later with a big smile on his face.

Nova had taken her turn then and dared Paisley to sneak into the admin offices and hide Mrs. Carey's favorite coffee mug. Paisley had gone one step further, stolen the coffee mug, and left a ransom note in its place.

Since then, the dares and the bets—the money and favors exchanged had started later, after they'd started college—had only gotten wilder.

Chantele leaned her elbows on the copper bar and tipped her head back to study the wooden rack that hung over the whole area. Chopped up bourbon bottles hanging from wire housed old-fashioned light bulbs—the kind that put out too little light to be much more than interesting.

The prerequisite mirror Chantele had come to expect behind every back bar in America was absent. In its place was an impressive display of liquor bottles, the lion's share of them being bourbon.

Welcome to Kentucky.

She'd come to the Bardstown area once before with her ex-boyfriend. Their relationship hadn't fared well on the Bourbon Trail, but damned if she hadn't loved the experience and the bourbon. She could thank John for that, she supposed.

A pour of Elijah Craig barrel proof or Old Ezra sounded good, but Chantele wasn't sure switching from her trusty old friend light beer to good, high proof bourbon was a wise move. Not when she was supposed to be seducing a cowboy.

Then again, maybe a little shot of something stiff and high proof was just exactly what she needed. Paisley was here. She would make sure Chantele and Nova didn't get black out drunk.

"Whatcha need?"

The bartender was easily six feet tall, bare arms covered in tattoos. Distracted by the ink on the woman's hands, it took Chantele a moment to focus and order.

"Just a gin and tonic," she finally found her voice, "and another longneck."

"Got it." The woman reached, grabbed a longneck from a cooler behind the bar, and popped the top off all without looking. Chantele could whip up a marketing plan for this bar that would rock all of Kentucky, but she couldn't do *that.* Impressed, she mumbled a thank you and took a long pull of her beer.

She turned to peek at the cowboy. He'd looked good from her seat at the table thirty minutes ago when he'd first walked in with his friend. Up close like this, Chantele might need a bar napkin to wipe up her drool. His hair—what she could see of it under his hat—was a mix of honey blond and caramel. Shirt sleeves rolled up over his wrists put his tan, sinewy forearms on display. He had big hands; she blushed again just imagining what Nova would say about that. No rings. No watch. Just a leather cord around his right wrist.

When the guy with him noticed her looking, Chantele nearly died of embarrassment. She felt flames shooting out her cheeks, and her knees went wobbly—less of a swoon and more of an *oh, shit, I'm dead* feeling.

Own this, Chan. If you're gonna seduce a guy this hot, you gotta play the part.

"Howdy."

The greeting from the other guy, the realization that she was watching them, turned her cowboy's lips up in a small smirk. Chantele wasn't impressed with the howdy. She wanted to ride a cowboy, not settle into *Green Acres* and meet people who loved farm livin'.

Still. The smirk on her cowboy's face was delicious and worth it.

"Hey." She gave them a polite nod.

Nova would be all over the guy by now. Paisley would play hard to get. Chantele still didn't know where she stood with guys and her friends and her mode of operation. Or maybe she just didn't have a modus operandi. Or mojo. Or whatever it was that had hooked Paisley a hot, devoted husband, and snagged any hot guy in the area to warm Nova's bed on her whims.

"You're not from around here."

Still the other guy talking.

Chantele glanced at the bartender when the woman gently shoved Nova's drink at her over the bar.

"Thanks."

"Where you from, darlin'?"

The guy doing all the talking was hot, but she decided he'd be more attractive if he stopped talking.

"Lexington," she answered, because why not? She wanted his friend to say something, so engaging in conversation with the talker was probably her best route.

"City girl." The smooth talker nodded. Chantele took another drink of her beer and turned to them, resting her right elbow on the bar. She wasn't completely helpless around men, but damned if she knew what to say.

"Anything fun to do around here?" she asked, channeling Nova.

"You're looking at it, honey."

Unsure if the guy was referring to drinking and dancing at the Iron Stag or himself, Chantele only nodded and gave them both the eye. Nova Brathewaite had that whole side-eye, once over down to an art; Chantele hoped she'd learned a little something from watching her friend through the years.

Her cowboy's smirk had grown into a real smile. The scruff around his mouth, the mustache, and the way his longish hair curled around the collar of his shirt was such a turn-on, Chantele felt her nipples harden under her silk tank.

Great.

They're not going to miss that.

As expected, the smooth-talker's eyes took a ride over her shoulders and lit up when he noticed the THO. He probably thought she was into him.

"You here alone, City Girl?"

"No," Chantele answered the talker, but her eyes were locked with her cowboy's warm, cognac-colored gaze. "Here with some friends."

She took another pull from her beer, feeling a jolt of lightning zing her tight little nipples all over again when the cowboy dropped his gaze to peek at her.

"You guys have a good night." She flicked her eyes over to the guy doing all the talking, but she was quick to look back at the cowboy. His eyebrows jumped a bit in surprise, but he held the smile and his tongue, and Chantele made her way back to her friends. She made sure to put a little swing in her step, laughing with her friends when she plopped back down in her chair.

“How’d it go?”

“No idea,” she answered. “But I could probably do the other one right there on the bar if I wanted to.”

“Yeah?” Paisley leaned a bit toward her to look at him around Nova.

“Don’t look!” Chantele shoved Paisley back gently.

“Careful, careful!” Paisley laughed. “The other guy was interested?”

“Yes, because I have a vagina.”

“Pretty sure guys don’t think of our kitties that way,” Nova mumbled with a pensive frown. “You’re not into him?”

“Nope.” Chantele shook her head. “His ego’s bigger than the state of Kentucky.”

“Yeah, but I wonder how big his cock is.”

Chantele choked on her beer and rolled her eyes at her friend. “I’m sure he’d show you.”

“I’m pretty sure I’ll ask.” Nova shrugged.

“Well, just so you know,” Paisley turned to Chantele with a frown, “Nova’s hookups here don’t get you out of the bet.”

“Hookups?” Nova yelped. “Plural?”

“Just sayin’,” Paisley answered with a grin.

CHAPTER TWO

RYE

Rye Gallagher was used to women coming onto his friend. Mav was like a damned magnet for all the hot girls. It had been that way as long as Rye could remember, starting with Sarah Beckoff announcing to her mom in first grade that she was going to marry Maverick Pressey. Rye doubted any woman was ever going to lasso Mav in and drag him to the altar, but he'd had more admirers and sex partners through the years than anyone else Rye knew. Mav's thick dark curls, bedroom eyes, and charm were hard to compete with, but when women learned *who* he was, or rather who *his father* was, there was no beating him.

Still, Rye turned and watched the strawberry blonde sashay across the bar to a table where two other women were waiting and watching her. The music was loud enough that he couldn't hear them, but they looked like they were laughing, teasing her. She'd probably said something about Mav and the other two had coaxed her up to the bar to get a round of drinks and talk to him while she was waiting.

Then again, the strawberry blonde hadn't made a direct play for Mav.

"Damn." Maverick's chuckle was as familiar to Rye as the sound of his own voice. "She's cute."

Not sure *cute* covered it, Rye studied her longer. The woman sitting beside her leaned into her and made a show of looking at them. Yep, the sexy little strawberry blonde had a thing for Mav. Rye, who wouldn't mind falling in love and settling down someday, was going to have to stop hanging out at the bar with his friend if he wanted to find love. Then again, maybe the Iron Stag wasn't the best place to look for wife material or love, anyway.

On the other hand, where else in Rodey was he going to meet women? Maybe the thrift store, but the last time he'd been inside that little hole-in-the-wall, the only women he'd seen had been old enough to be his mother. Church, he supposed. Rye didn't make it as faithfully as he should, but even if he did, he didn't think church was a good place to look for love, either. Not the kind of love he wanted.

"She'll be back," Mav announced.

She would, too. Rye knew that. The girl would venture back up to the bar and order another round. This time, she'd inch in a bit closer—maybe to him, maybe to Mav—and she'd talk a bit more. Play with the label on her bottle and make bedroom eyes at Mav. And before long, they'd be heading out the door and leaving Rye standing here at the bar with Marlowe. Not that he minded; he and Marlowe could shut the place down drinking and talking on opposite sides of the bar.

But just once, Rye would like to get the girl.

At the table, the three women were laughing again. Rye huffed out a sigh, ready to hit Marlowe up for another beer. Maybe he'd drink one more and then order a burger. Get home and hit the sack early. Sometimes it was hard to believe he and Maverick Pressey were the same age. Rye was usually in bed by ten and up at dawn and ready to work. Mav rarely made it in before midnight, and most nights that was generous. The guy had bedded damned near every woman in Rodey and the surrounding twenty-five-mile radius.

He was never late to work; Robert Pressey wouldn't allow that. But there were mornings when Mav slipped into the main barn by the skin of his teeth, missing mucking the stalls by a tenth of a second. Robert expected just as much from his own son as he did everyone else who worked on the ranch.

The blonde across the table from Shortcake pushed her chair back and unfolded slowly. Tall and lean with just the right amount of curve in all the right places, she stood for a moment talking and finally turned around. Blond ringlets framed her face, probably escapees from the clip at the back of her head, but also probably escapees on purpose. Rye saw far too many women with that whole wispy curl thing to think it was less than a style.

Mav cut loose a low grumble of appreciation as the tall blonde walked away from the table and headed for the ladies' room. Rye laughed good-naturedly when she turned toward them and gifted Mav with a bold stare. So, it was going to be one of those kind of nights for his friend; Rye was used to that, too. Both women—hell, who knew, maybe the third one would join them, too—were going to leave the bar with Maverick tonight.

As he'd done several times before, Mav would invite Rye to join them. Aside from the fact that Rye wasn't big on the idea of somehow ending up skin-to-skin with Maverick, he wasn't sure he wanted that kind of thing anyway. He wasn't a saint, by any means, and if he were being honest, he'd found himself in bed with two women at a time once or twice when he was fresh out of high school and utterly unable to impress both women in one night. That part would be different now that he was older, a little more mature, and a little more in control of himself.

But Rye didn't want a night of steamy, empty sex with one, two, or three pretty girls.

He wanted more.

"Did you hear Kenny Atley's dad died?"

Rye glanced at his friend, a little bit relieved to move on from the threesome in the works. Too bad the distraction was sad news.

"Nope."

The two of them turned back to the bar. Kenny Atley was another classmate of theirs; his dad had been fighting cancer for a long time. The news wasn't shocking, just sad. Rye's parents were nearing their 60s, but he knew better than to think that youth meant good health.

"Don't you guys ever get tired of hanging out here?"

Rye flicked his gaze up as Marlowe slid by them behind the bar, scooped up another bottled beer, opened it, and turned away to deliver said bottle to a customer down the line.

"Where else are we gonna hang out, Mar?" Rye asked when she moved back their way.

The woman snagged a glass of ice water from the back bar and took a long drink.

"We're in the heart of bourbon country," she reminded them. "I'll say it again. *Bourbon country*. And you guys come in here night after night for light beer."

"You think I can afford to hit those fancy distillery bars for a two-finger pour of the good stuff every night?" Rye tipped his head and narrowed his eyes at her.

"You sayin' I'm cheap entertainment?" She threw a smirk his way.

They'd dated. If you counted going to a movie, grabbing a beer, and going out for pizza as dating. They'd made out once, too. Far enough to get each other off. But not far enough to hurt each other. And then they'd decided they were better friends than anything else. Rye was happy with their choice.

See? Maturity. He didn't know about Marlowe Dailey, but he'd matured a lot since his teens and early twenties.

"I'm watchin' my figure," Mav told her. Marlowe, eyes still locked with Rye's, snorted and nodded.

"Watchin' those figure eights you do in bed, maybe."

"Figure eights?" Rye swung his gaze from Marlowe to Mav and back again. "What—?"

"Women talk," Marlowe reminded them. "And I'm a bartender, boys. I hear it all."

Rye wondered if that meant she'd heard about his night with Evie Carter a few months ago. *Wham, bam, thank you, man*—Evie had climbed him like a fucking tree, impaled herself on his dick, and bounced on him like he was a kid's rocking horse. With her obscene tits as big as melons in his face, he'd come two minutes in, and Evie had followed about three seconds later.

Before he could even request a second round, she'd dismounted, pulled her skirt down, smacked a quick kiss on the corner of his mouth, and promised him she'd see him later.

"Can I get another?" He pushed his bottle at Marlowe, unable to meet her eyes. *Women talk.* Not a new concept, but damned if that didn't just smack him right between the eyes. True, Evie Carter was the female equivalent of Maverick Pressey, and everyone knew it. Even Evie. Everyone loved her, just as everyone loved Mav.

But that didn't mean Rye was happy about how that night turned out.

"Buy me a drink."

It wasn't a question. Not even a suggestion, really.

Rye glanced at Mav only to find that tall blonde with the curly wispy hair around her face standing by him.

Mav glanced at Marlowe with a shrug. Still a little sensitive after the reminder that Marlowe probably knew as much about everyone here as a psychiatrist or a priest, Rye avoided her eyes and watched the blonde instead.

"Gin and tonic," the blonde told her with a warm smile.

"I'm Mav."

"Of course you are," she answered with a hearty laugh. "Nova."

"This is my friend, Rye." Mav nodded at him.

The woman tipped her head to Rye. "Hey."

Marlowe mixed the gin and tonic, stuck a straw in the glass, and handed it to Nova.

"How about a dance?"

"Yeah. Sounds good."

Rye watched Mav trail the blonde to the crowded dance floor, his hand already resting possessively on the small of her back. When Rye turned back to the bar, Marlowe had moved to make another drink for someone else. Rye picked up his fresh beer for a drink, wondering which of the women hot for him Mav would do first.

CHAPTER THREE

Chantele

"Let's go!" Paisley grabbed for Chantele's hand as she scooted her chair back and stood up. Ready to get up and move a bit after watching Nova dance with her cowboy's friend, Chantele kicked her own chair out of the way and followed Paisley to the dance floor. Apparently, most of the folks in the Iron Stag liked "Fancy Like" as most of the tables emptied, and people flocked to the dance floor.

Like riding a bike, the steps to the line dance she'd done a hundred times came back to Chantele as she and Paisley took their place on the floor, a few lines behind Nova and the guy. Chantele hoped her cowboy was somewhere watching, since she couldn't find him on the dance floor.

She'd dressed a little revealing—at her friends' prompting—and she could shake her ass as Paisley said. But none of that mattered if she hadn't made enough of an impression on the cowboy for him to be looking now. The ironic thing was that Nova had a sure thing there with her dance partner, but the chips were down for Chantele. If she didn't ride a cowboy before this weekend was over, she owed Nova and Paisley six months' worth of making weekend breakfasts and coffees. And yes, cooking for Paisley also meant cooking for her husband, Vince.

Big and wide like a lineman, Vince liked to eat.

They stayed on the floor, and Nova eventually joined them. When a Guns 'N Roses song started, they huddled up and danced together.

"I think he's watching you." Paisley danced closer to Chantele.

"I know how to make sure you have his attention."

Chantele turned to Nova. "What?" She grabbed her friend's hands to force her to focus.

"Ride the bull."

"Excuse me?" Chantele asked with a frown.

"Ride the bull."

"Nope."

"Seriously?" Paisley whooped. "There's a mechanical bull here?"

"Stop it!" Chantele let go of Nova only to launch herself at Paisley. "Stop! Shhh!"

"My friend Mav says there is." Nova nodded.

"Mav?" Paisley repeated.

"Short for Maverick," Nova explained. She still swayed her hips to the music, and Chantele thought she still looked sexy as hell. Something she didn't think she could pull off in a million years. Not even if she did shake her ass and her tits. For all she knew, all she would have to show for this circus getup tomorrow was sore boobs from lack of support.

"Wow." Paisley nodded. "Okay. So. Where's the bull?"

"I'm not riding a bull."

"Back corner over there." Nova nodded to the far, dark corner of the bar.

"Shit." Chantele wouldn't have paid a bit of attention to the mechanical bull if Nova hadn't brought it up. A spotlight hung directly above the damned thing, but it was currently turned off. In fact, Chantele wondered if—hoped—it was out of commission.

"I mentioned to Mav that we might like to give it a shot."

"Are you serious?" Chantele lunged at Nova now.

"So serious."

"He said he'd talk to Marlowe, and she'd talk to James."

"Who the fuck are Marlowe and James? Some new flavored liquor or something?"

"Watch the language," Paisley said to Chantele with a wink. "Little ears."

Chantele rolled her eyes when Paisley touched her belly.

"And yet, you're content to talk about me riding a cowboy. Your baby's gonna hear that, too."

"That's different," Paisley said with a shrug.

"I'll do it if you do it," Nova told Chantele.

"You will?"

"Yeah." Nova shrugged like climbing up on the back of a mechanical bucking bull in front of a room packed with strangers was no big deal.

"Okay." Chantele pursed her lips. She needed to get that guy's attention somehow. For one thing, she didn't *want* to be on breakfast duty, weekend or not. And another? After getting that close-up look at him, her girl parts which had been on an extended vacation were raring to get busy. Another drink or two, and she might just climb on and ride him, with or without the bet hanging over her head.

"But you're gonna have to go first," Nova continued.

"What?"

Her friend shrugged and looked over Chantele's shoulder, a smile lighting up her face.

"Shit." Chantele locked eyes with a now grinning Paisley.

"Gotta round of tequila shots here for you ladies."

Chantele jerked her gaze to Nova when the smooth-talking ladies' man appeared at their sides. Nova took hers and knocked it back instantly. Running a hand over her mouth, she eyed Mav and handed the empty shot glass back to him. When Nova shot Chantele a commanding look, she took a glass and threw the clear liquor back easily.

Mav glanced at Paisley suggestively.

"Pregnant," she answered with a shake of her head. "But Chan'll do it."

"Chan." Mav nodded and traded glasses with Chantele.

Well, damn. Hadn't she just had the thought that after two more drinks, she might be skipping right over the bull and climbing the cowboy?

Maybe she'd have to do the bull first, and then when Nova climbed on, she could make her move with the cowboy. She tossed the second shot back as easily as the first and tried not to think about the three beers she'd already downed.

"Hey, Iron Stag!"

A male voice blared from a speaker system, a bit contorted and hard to hear with the music still blaring. Chantele's belly buzzed like she'd swallowed a beehive as she locked eyes with Nova. She'd done some crazy things in her lifetime, but she'd never ridden a bull. Mechanical or not. She'd never even been on the back of a horse.

"We got some little ladies who wanna ride Ol' Bogart! C'mon over, ladies!"

The crowd at the bar hooted with delight, egging Nova on. Chantele's slice of bravery from a moment ago vanished as Nova and Paisley took her hands and led her to the bull in the corner.

"This is Bogart." Maverick rested his hand on the bull's head. "Who's first?"

Chantele couldn't find her voice to say a word—not to say she was first or to argue with Nova that she didn't want to go first. Nova nodded her head at Chantele when Maverick looked at her.

Feeling all kinds of eyes on her, Chantele resisted the urge to crane her neck around to see if she could find her cowboy watching. Once she saw everyone tuned into her and this damned bull, she would lose her nerve. The cowboy she had her eyes on would leave unimpressed, and she would be scouring the internet for interesting breakfast casseroles.

"You want me to show you how it's done?" Maverick folded his arms over his chest and tipped his head at her. Put off by this guy's cocky attitude, Chantele wanted to say no. But then again, there was that pesky little problem of never having been on horseback, let alone a bucking bull.

"I think that sounds like a great idea."

Chantele glanced at Nova. Her friend wasn't hoping for this guy to show them the ropes; Nova wanted to see him ride. She wanted to see the suggestive hip thrusts and rolls.

"Okay." Maverick nodded and walked over to the sound booth at the back of the place. Chantele watched him talk to the guy there—she assumed it was either Marlowe or James—and then glanced at Nova.

"I think you're gonna owe me for this," she decided.

"Watchin' that body on the bull?" Nova asked with a dramatic frown.

"Making me ride the bull."

Nova laughed softly and shook her head. "Just don't sit there rigid."

"Have you done it before?"

"No, but I've watched." Nova cleared her throat. "A lot of guys. A lot of people. You gotta be loose to hold your balance."

"Great." Chantele nodded as the guy in the sound booth stepped out and approached her and her friends.

"Hey ladies." He offered them a smile. This guy was older, probably late fifties or early sixties. Still nice-looking. Same beat up old boots every other guy in the place wore. His graying hair was smashed down a bit, as if he had been wearing a hat at some point tonight. "Need you to sign a disclaimer first."

Nova grinned at him and grabbed the pen. Chantele held her breath as her friend scribbled her name on the paper and then winked at her. Chantele took the pen and signed her name, flicking her eyes up when someone else walked by the bull.

Bogart. Why the hell was this bull's name Bogart?

Her heart ramped up and banged around like an amateur drummer doing a solo. Her cowboy was standing with Maverick now. She felt her face flush when their eyes met.

Well, okay, now that he was over here, and she knew he was watching, she was all in.

Maverick returned to stand with her and Nova as Paisley edged away to stand with Chantele's cowboy.

"Okay." The guy's gaze lingered on Nova longer, but he eventually looked at Chantele with a grin. "The flooring here around Bogart's padded. So, when you fall, it's not gonna be that bad."

Chantele shot Nova a look. Her friend's eyes narrowed at his use of the word *when* instead of *if.*

"But also, you're gonna use that to get on the ol' boy. 'Kay? It's gonna bounce, give you a boost up." When she and Nova nodded, he continued. "You're gonna hold onto that rope there palm up with your nondominant hand."

"Why wouldn't you hold on with your stronger hand?" Chantele asked him.

"Well, you can," Maverick answered with a shrug. "But I feel like the dominant hand is better freed for balance."

Chantele decided he had a point, but he looked so smug, she hated to admit it.

"You ride a lot of bulls, do you?"

He grinned. "A few. But I know a guy who used to. Learned a lot from Taj Bailey."

"You know Taj Bailey?" Nova sounded surprised.

"I do." The guy nodded. "Nice guy. He ain't rodeoin' anymore. Some nice girl settled his ass down good and hard."

Chantele rolled her eyes when Maverick said the words and looked pointedly at Nova.

"I thought he quit a while back." She tipped her head, thrilled to catch his error. "Injuries."

"He did," Maverick agreed. "But then he met a nice girl, and now he's got another baby on the way."

"You know him that well?" Nova asked.

"You one of those girls who likes to break up a good thing, honey?" Maverick asked her.

"No." She shook her head. "I'm just impressed."

"Lemme just show you something to be impressed about." He winked at her again. Chantele shot a peek at Paisley and rolled her eyes.

CHAPTER FOUR

Rye

"Seems like maybe he's done this before."

Rye took his eyes off his buddy rolling his hips on Bogart like he was riding the flavor of the day. The third woman in the group stood at his side with a grin. She was cute, too, with short, spiky brown hair and big brown eyes. Unlike the other two, she wore a wedding ring.

"Time or two." Rye looked back at Maverick with a nod. He waved his right hand in the air, keeping his body loose as Bogart tried to throw him.

"I'm Paisley."

"Rye," he offered, wondering what the strawberry blonde's name was.

"This is supposed to be a girls' weekend." Paisley glanced longingly toward the bar where Marlowe was talking up yet another cowboy. "My last before this baby is too big for me to move comfortably."

"You're having a baby?" Rye jumped to attention. "Do you wanna sit down? Are you okay?"

"Relax." Paisley reached to pat his arm. "I'm not very far along. I'm fine. The point being I can't even nurse a beer while these two are shooting tequila."

Maverick hopped off Bogart with ease when his time was up.

"Oh man." Paisley shook her head and trilled a sweet laugh when Maverick said something to the girl Rye had been watching.

"Has she ridden before?"

"Maybe an elephant at the circus when she was five."

Rye snorted at the unexpected sarcasm.

"Motorcycle."

"She rides a motorcycle?"

"She has," Paisley told him. "Chantele dated a guy with a Harley before."

Rodey, we have a name.

Rye arranged his face in what he hoped was a blank, nonchalant look. *Chantele.* He liked her. Wouldn't mind dancing with her. Too bad she'd made her move for Maverick. Rye just wasn't much for sharing.

Over by Bogart, Chantele nodded and giggled, reaching for Nova's arm to steady herself.

"How about the blonde?"

"Nova," Paisley told him. "Not afraid of anything."

That seemed about right, just from what he'd seen of the woman tonight.

Maverick bounced on the pad around Bogart, eyes on Chantele, as he talked. Rye saw him instructing her again on the rope and how to hold on. When he waved his hand in the air, Rye knew he was telling her to use her free arm for balance.

"Rye." Rye snapped to attention when Maverick called his name. "She needs a hat."

"What?"

"The lady needs a hat."

"Mav, the last damned thing this lady wants is my sweaty hat on her head." Rye jerked his head out of Mav's reach, but damned if Mav didn't move with him and snatch the damned thing off him.

"There ya go." Mav put the hat on Chantele's head and gave her the once over. He nodded in approval and stepped back. "Okay. Just hold on and stay loose. When Bogart rears his head, you lean forward. Got it?"

"Yep."

Rye couldn't swear to it because he wasn't standing close enough to be sure. But he thought Chantele's eyes were glassy. He had no idea how long she'd been here or what she'd had to drink before he noticed her. But she'd just shot a beer and two pours of tequila, so odds were, she might be seeing two Mavericks and two Bogarts at the moment.

"Is she okay?" Rye asked her friend Paisley. "She's not drunk, is she?"

"Tipsy," Paisley answered. "This weekend might be for me, but I'm always the responsible one." She cut her eyes to Rye and stared him down. "I'm not gonna let her do something stupid."

Rye wondered if that included not letting her leave with Maverick when her ride was over—no matter how it ended. And he wondered if Paisley had the same kind of control over Nova. Something told him that would be a no.

Chantele glanced at Nova and then looked back at Bogart. She bounced hard on the pad, jumped, and missed, her body sliding back down the same side she stood on.

"Ouch." Paisley snorted.

Chantele seemed undeterred. She giggled loud enough that Rye heard her and then gave it another try. This time, she got her right leg up and over Bogart and used her hands to right herself. James called to her, asked if she was ready. When she blew out a big huff and glanced at Rye, he held his breath. He'd never paid a dime's worth of attention to anyone on Bogart before, other than the nights he and Mav were here with a big group of friends, and they all drank enough to decide they were bored and wanted some adventure. Around Rodey, the mechanical bull and the distilleries *were* the big adventures.

When Bogart started moving, Chantele wobbled a bit but managed to settle for a moment. The blonde—Nova—had wandered back over to stand by the pregnant friend.

"I think she's drunk," Nova announced.

"Drunk enough to get hurt?" Rye leaned in to ask.

"I thought drunk people didn't get hurt as badly in accidents as sober people."

Paisley rolled her eyes at Nova and looked back at Rye.

"She's tipsy. She's not drunk. She's had a few beers and those two shots."

That made Rye feel somewhat better. Didn't seem like that much, but then again, he didn't know these women well enough to have the slightest idea how much any of them could handle. Nova let out a loud whoop, followed by a hearty laugh. Rye turned his eyes back to the girl on the bull. She was flopped over the side, head close to Bogart's like she was telling him a secret.

"She's cracking up."

Rye saw Paisley elbow Nova.

"I'm gonna pee my pants just watchin' her," Nova howled with laughter.

The girl on the bull tried to straighten, but within a second, she was off the bull and splattered on the pads around it.

"You okay?" Maverick offered her a hand. Still laughing, Chantele put her hand in his and let him pull her up.

"I'm good." She nodded, but she turned to look at Nova. "Your turn."

"You didn't give me much to beat." Nova eyed her friend with a sloppy grin. "You wanna wager—"

"No."

Chantele's loud answer didn't seem to bother Nova. She simply approached the bull, shot Mav a sultry look, and climbed up on Bogart's back like she was raised on a horse ranch.

"She ride?" Rye asked Paisley in disbelief.

"She has," Paisley answered.

"Bulls?"

"No."

"Please." Chantele snorted. "She's afraid of cats."

"She looks pretty smokin' hot on that bull, Chan."

"She does," Chantele agreed. Her cheeks were pink as she looked over her shoulder, but Rye figured that was adrenaline rather than embarrassment.

"Thirsty?" He tipped his head at her. Lightning zapped him right in the heart when their eyes met. Damn, she was cute *and* pretty, and if he'd never known the difference before, he sure as hell did now.

"Yes."

"Beer?"

"Please." She nodded. "I—"

He smiled and cut her off. "I know what you were drinking."

CHAPTER FIVE

CHANTELE

"Are you really okay?"

Chantele flicked her eyes to Paisley but quickly looked back at Nova. Damned if she didn't move on the back of that bull like she'd grown up in rodeo. *Stripper* rodeo. Nova's moves were so sexy, so suggestive, that Chantele couldn't even be frustrated with her friend for upstaging her. She was too tuned into the show.

"She ever loses her job, she could waitress at Gilley's," she told Paisley. "I'm fine. This bitch is killin' my pride, but I'll live."

"Worth it, though." Paisley elbowed her with a laugh. "He noticed you."

"Yeah, well, let's hope she's off Bogart before he comes back with my beer, or she's gonna be tag-teaming the cowboys while you and I go back to the house and watch The Game Show Network."

Paisley snorted. From the corner of her eye, Chantele saw her friend shake her head.

"Your boobs looked good up there," Paisley told her.

"Yeah?" Chantele quirked an eyebrow and turned to her hopefully.

"Yeah. For that half a second turn when you were waving his hat."

"Shit." Chantele giggled and pulled his hat off her head. She'd lost it when she fell off Bogart but snatched it off the pads when she climbed quickly to her feet. It hadn't crossed her mind to give it back to the guy, not even when he'd gone off to get her a beer. "What's his name?"

"Rye."

She spun around when she heard his voice behind her. Nova finally spilled off the bull, crashing to the pads on the other side. Chantele held her breath for a second, but she let it go when she heard her friend laughing. Paisley excused herself and slipped around Bogart to check on her.

"Rye." Chantele nodded and focused on the cowboy as he passed her a longneck. "Well."

"Looks better on you," he said with a grin when she leaned close and set the hat back on his head. "Sorry Mav insisted on that."

She shrugged. "I didn't mind."

Maybe she couldn't ride a damned bucking bull like Nova, but she had a decent body, and she knew how to get what she wanted. Rye gave her a small nod as she took a drink of her beer.

"Thank you." She licked her lips. "For the beer."

"No problem." Rye peeked over his shoulder, and Chantele leaned around him to watch Mav and Paisley help a still laughing Nova stand up. "Don't worry."

Chantele jerked her gaze from Nova back to her cowboy. "I'm not at all worried. What should I be worried about?"

"Mav doesn't choose," Rye told her. "The more, the merrier for him."

Chantele laughed softly. "Perfect match for Nova, then."

With his back to the bull, Rye rested his elbows on the wooden railing around the area. "And you?"

Realization dawned; he was telling her not to worry about Mav paying attention to Nova. As if he thought she was into Maverick. Damn. Maybe he had assumed she was making eyes at Maverick when she'd approached the bar earlier to order.

If that was the case, maybe she did have a lot to learn about flirting with a guy. Yes, she'd talked to Maverick, but only because he was the one doing the talking.

"No." She turned her back to the bull and leaned gingerly on the railing, but she kept her eyes on him.

"So, you're gonna be one of them who turns him down because—"

Chantele leaned closer to him and before she realized what she was doing, she snaked her hand around the back of his neck and tugged his face down to kiss him. She hadn't kissed anyone in a good month or two or maybe even six, but like riding a bike or tasting a favorite sweet, it all came back to her as her cowboy turned to her and slid his fingers over her hip. She smoothed her lips over his once and again, breathing deep to draw his scent in. Outdoors. Cedar. And beer. All of it together was masculine and heady and drove her back to press her lips to his again. This time, she dragged her teeth over his lower lip, thrilled when he groaned in delight. Before he could change his mind, Chantele swept her tongue between his lips. The slide of his tongue over hers chased a spark through her veins.

She was a little bit surprised when she drew back and opened her eyes. For a second, she had been all alone with her cowboy, lost in that kiss, and the rest of the world had been paused and quiet. Now, eyes locked with his, the music pounded around them again. Chantele wasn't sure she would have said "Boot Scootin' Boogie" was a sexy song, but damned if Brooks and Dunn didn't make her want to latch onto Rye and kiss him again.

"Not into Maverick," she said with a little shrug.

Rye quirked an eyebrow at her as he lifted his bottle to his lips for a drink.

"Wanna dance?" he asked just as the song ended, and something slow started.

"Sure."

When he held out his hand, Chantele linked her fingers with his and followed him back past Bogart and her friends to the dance floor. Rye hooked his arms around her waist and pulled her in close as Alison Kraus' voice surrounded them. Chantele looped her arms around his neck, her beer still in hand.

"Lexington, huh?"

"Mmm." She nodded. "From Indiana, but I live in Lexington now."

"What brings you to Rodey?"

"Bourbon trail," she answered with a shrug. "What else?"

"You're a bourbon drinker?" He narrowed his eyes at her suspiciously.

"Mm. Well." She tipped her head. "I like bourbon, but on the other hand, this trip is supposed to be all about Paisley."

Rye nodded as if he wanted her to keep talking.

"Kind of a big hurrah before she's too pregnant to do stuff." Chantele couldn't tell him that part of the trip was about her finding a cowboy to ride before she and her friends went home. "So...even though we're in bourbon country, I'm not sure Paisley would appreciate it if Nova and I got bombed on bourbon."

"What's your favorite?"

"Testing me?"

Again, he quirked an eyebrow at her and waited for her to answer him.

"I don't know that I have a favorite," she finally mumbled. Before he could comment—she sensed a mansplaining moment coming from the look on his face—she shook her head and put her finger over his lips. "But my go-to right now is Elijah Craig barrel proof."

"Barrel proof?" He drew back in surprise.

"Yeah."

"Ever had Lockland?"

"No."

"They're right here in Rodey."

"Let me guess." She sighed softly when he pressed his palm against her butt. "Mm. Nice. You work at Lockland?"

"Nope." He grinned. "But they have good whiskey."

"'kay."

Suddenly, her cowboy whirled her around, slid his fingers down her arm and took her hand, and pulled her off the dance floor. The song changed as they walked off. Chantele wondered if Rye practiced his timing or if he just didn't care for Billy Ray Cyrus.

"What're we doing?"

"You." He glanced back over his shoulder and met her eyes. "Are gonna put your money where your mouth is."

He led her to the bar and slid his hand over her waist again when she stood beside him. Chantele leaned into him, thrilled both at the thought of getting familiar with his hard body and not having to do weekend breakfasts for the next six months.

"Marlowe." Rye stuck a finger in Chantele's belt loop and gave her a possessive yank to draw her even closer. "My friend here would like a pour of Elijah Craig barrel proof."

"Rocks?" The tall bartender arched her brows at Chantele as she splashed vodka into the silver jigger in her hands.

"Neat."

Marlowe gave her a nod of approval. "Just one second."

CHAPTER SIX

RYE

Even Marlowe stopped moving long enough to watch Chantele take her first sip of the Elijah Craig. Rye watched her closely, impressed when she nosed the whiskey just the way the experts instructed. She sipped the amber liquor, held it on her tongue—even chewed it—and closed her eyes. When she swallowed, she opened her eyes to look at him.

"Mmm." She offered him a smile and tipped the glass to him.

"What do you like about it?" he asked her.

"The taste," she answered easily. "And the bite."

Rye took a sip of the bourbon and handed the Glen Cairn glass back to her.

"You like a little bite, huh?"

Chantele snorted softly. "Who doesn't like a little bite now and then?"

"You'd be surprised," he mumbled.

"What'd you think?" Marlowe reappeared across the bar and drummed her fingers as she looked back and forth between them.

"That one's her go-to," Rye told Marlowe, eyes still on Chantele. "Let's try a pour of Lockland."

"Five year?" Marlowe was turning away to grab the bottle as Rye nodded.

Chantele twisted around to eyeball the dance floor, probably looking for her friends.

"Do you wanna go tell them where you are?" he asked when she turned back to the bar.

"Nope." She shook her head. "They'll figure it out."

Marlowe pushed a new glass over the bar toward Chantele. Again, she swirled the amber liquor in the glass and then nosed it before sipping.

"Where'd you learn how to drink bourbon?"

"Seriously?" She lowered the glass and gave him the side eye.

"What?" Rye gave her a dramatic shrug, uncomfortable with the frown she wore.

"Are you suggesting that because I'm a woman I shouldn't know how to drink bourbon?"

"Look around, Chantele." He leaned in close and nodded his head toward the tables behind them. "There are a lot of women here. And there are a lot of women in Kentucky who know how to drink bourbon."

She opened her mouth; the sharp look on her face suggested she was going to rail on him again. He shook his head and pressed his thumb to her lips before she could speak.

"There are also a lot of guys in Kentucky who *don't* know how to drink bourbon." He shrugged again. "I'm not suggesting a little lady like you shouldn't know how to drink whiskey."

"A guy I dated was a bourbon drinker." She spoke quietly as if his explanation had smoothed her ruffled feathers.

"Same guy who rode the Harley?"

She snapped her gaze up to look at him. "What? How do you know—? Paisley."

Rye laughed softly. "You gonna try that?" He nodded at the glass in her hand; she still hadn't tried the Lockland.

"Why did she tell you about Johnny?"

"Johnny," Rye repeated absently as she lifted the glass to nose the bourbon again. Marlowe shot him a grin as she slid down the bar. Rye shoved down the thoughts of girls, women, he'd dated and or slept with standing here at the bar, spilling their guts to his friend Marlowe, and watched as Chantele finally sipped the Lockland five year. No, he didn't work there, but he knew the Lockland family well. He and Maverick had gone to school with Knox Lockland. They'd all had a crush on Knox's little sister Summer—the very same woman who had tamed Taj Bailey, the former champion bull rider.

He wasn't sure why it mattered that Chantele liked the Lockland. Sure, he could claim a few degrees of separation, but on the other hand, would he see her after tonight? She'd made her interest in him clear, and that kiss, her declaration, that she wasn't into Maverick, had been like a damned firecracker exploding in his gut. But no matter what happened tonight, would he see her again? Did he want something quick and easy? Something that might be exciting as fuck and even fancy to look at that would fade away just as quickly as fireworks?

Maverick would give him shit about it, but no, that's not what Rye wanted. For fuck's sake, if he wanted a night of easy, steamy sex, there were girls he could call. Friends with benefits right here around Rodey.

"Oh." Chantele nodded. She looked up at him, brows raised and her lips curved in a small smile. "Yeah. That's good."

"Tell me about Johnny." Rye eased back onto the barstool behind him, pulling her with him. Nope, his heart wasn't into the idea of a hookup, but his dick was. For now, the rest of him would ride along and see where tonight led. Get to know her. See if anything could come of this. Her life in Lexington might be a world away from his, but Lexington itself was barely an hour away.

With a soft sigh, Chantele turned sideways at the bar to face him. For a second, she eyed the liquor still in the glass as she twirled it, but finally, she lifted her gaze to his. She knew how to play the game; Rye would give her that. Maybe she wasn't as blatantly sexy as her friend Nova, but there was something about her that was already under his skin.

“There’s really not much to tell.” She shrugged. “We dated.”

“For how long?”

“Couple of years.”

“Seems like a lot to tell about a relationship that lasted a couple of years.”

“I mean, if you want to know that he watched TV while he brushed his teeth...That he liked grape soda...Drove a semi for a year when he was twenty-seven but quit for a job in a warehouse...And likes pecan pie...” She shrugged again.

“Who doesn’t like pecan pie?” Rye shook his head.

“Me.”

“I’m sorry. Did you say you live in Kentucky?”

She laughed softly.

“What’d he look like?”

Chantele sipped her whiskey again and tipped her head. “Why would that matter?”

“Just curious.”

“He had long blond hair. Wore it in a ponytail most of the time.”

“How’d that work with a helmet?”

This time, the sound that bubbled out of her was a loud, raucous belly-laugh.

“Were you in love?”

“Yeah.” She nodded. “We were. But not enough. Not for the long haul.”

“What’s your long haul look like?”

“I feel like I’m on a job interview.”

“Where you’re drinking bourbon.” Rye pointed at her glass with a grin. “I’d apply for that job.”

“My long haul.” She took a deep breath and pursed her lips, lost in thought.

CHAPTER SEVEN

CHANTELE

Marriage and kids. *That* was her long haul. But most guys in bars didn't want to hear that, did they? Then again, Chantele wasn't sure guys in bars wanted to hear about career aspirations or travel wish lists, either. Guys in bars, guys buying girls drinks in bars, wanted one thing, right?

Which would be convenient because she wanted that one thing very much, too.

"Gonna make me guess?" he asked.

Chantele took another peek at the dance floor. When she didn't see her friends, she looked back at their table, relieved to see both Paisley and Nova there. She didn't care if Nova hooked up with Mav, but she didn't want to leave Paisley stranded by herself, either. Thankfully, Nova felt the same.

"I'm curious what you see my long haul to be." She looked back at Rye.

"Okay." He nodded. "I think you are...in sales. And you're very good at it. You're a career woman. Guessing you're not quite thirty, and you're looking to settle down with a professional one day. You'll get married. You're going to live in a townhouse. You and your husband will read the paper every Sunday. You'll drink bougie coffee while you're out walking your dogs, and you'll do things like art galleries and gala events for fundraisers."

Chantele studied his face for a moment. A mix of amusement and indignation roiled inside her. The bar crowd suddenly felt much too loud; the pounding beat of an Alabama song only making it feel worse.

Did she really want to sleep with this guy? First the question about bourbon. And now his future cast putting her in a townhouse drinking bougie coffee?

"So?" He raised his eyebrows in askance. Chantele frowned when he lifted a longneck to his lips for a drink. When had he ordered another beer? "Am I right?"

"No, actually."

"About which part?"

"Most of it." She shrugged.

"Come with me." He slid off the stool, his thigh solid and warm against her as he bumped her to scoot her out of his way. She let him hook her fingers again and followed him to the main entrance. Was he taking her outside to put the moves on her? Would she let him?

Chantele eyed his ass as she followed. Paisley was more of a suit and tie kind of girl. Nova wasn't choosy. Chantele liked guys rough and worn, casual and comfortable. She preferred denim to suits. Thermal shirts to button-downs. Hair a little wild, in need of a trim, to the corporate cut. And scruff to clean-shaven.

This guy ticked all those boxes.

She didn't have to like him to hook up with him. That wasn't part of the bet. For that matter, she could lie to her girlfriends. But she wouldn't.

Did that say something about her? The fact that she would rather use a guy for sex to win a bet with her friends than lie to her friends about said dare?

Diamonds dotted a black sky above them as Rye led her to a picnic table out behind the building. She could still hear Alabama, but the music was far away now, tucked inside the Iron Stag. She heard voices, too, but they were muffled. Maybe someone in the parking lot. Maybe someone out for a cigarette, phone call, or something a little more personal.

"I didn't hear you order another beer," she mumbled as they climbed up to sit on the table.

"Didn't." He shrugged. "Marlowe and I are friends."

"So you drink free?"

"No." He snorted softly. "But she's good at reading my mind."

Chantele took the bottle when he handed it to her and took a drink.

"Did you want another one?" he asked suddenly. "Happy to grab you another."

"Probably shouldn't." She smiled. Their fingers brushed when he took the bottle back from her.

"Tell me." He leaned forward and rested his elbows on his knees.

"Not in sales. Not not quite thirty. I don't understand a damned thing about abstract art. And I don't drink bougie coffee."

"How do you take your coffee?"

"Black."

"What do you do?"

Chantele mimicked his pose as she studied him. "I'm still trying to decide if I should be offended by your future cast for me."

"What?" The brim of his hat hid the frown, but Chantele knew from his tone that it was there. "Why would you be offended?"

"I'm thirty-two. I work in marketing."

"Close to sales."

"Eh." She shrugged. "I do a lot of graphic design, but as I said, I don't get abstract art. I *am* a dog person."

"That's the only thing I got right?"

She licked her lips and narrowed her eyes in thought. "Um. I read the news, but not faithfully. I like to be informed, but also, the news usually sucks, and I'm a positive person. I do give to a lot of fundraisers, but the last time I was at a gala was about seven years ago. It was a thing for my dad."

"What kind of dog?"

"I have an Aussie German shepherd."

"Named Batman."

"No." She laughed and rolled her eyes. "You're really bad at this."

The way he smiled at her was like striking a match. Heat flooded her from her heart to her toes.

"Might be good at other things." He tipped his head back far enough that she saw him arch his brows suggestively.

"What's your long haul?"

"We ain't got yours figured out yet, darlin'."

If that smile hadn't sparked a flame, his voice and the word *darlin'* sure as hell did it. Chantele huffed out a quick breath and looked away.

"I like my job. I do want to settle down. My brother and his wife have four kids. I'd like at least one before I'm dead. And no. Just no. On the townhouse."

"Horses?"

"Love them, but I don't have a horse," she answered. "Nor does anyone in my family. As you probably figured out when I couldn't even get on that damned bull in there."

"Paisley says you rode an elephant when you were five."

Chantele laughed softly and rolled her eyes. "Sounds like you and Paisley had quite a conversation."

"If you had to choose between the circus and an art gallery, which would you choose?"

"Art gallery," she answered with a tiny shrug. "I don't like clowns. The acrobats make me jealous. And I think circus people are cruel to animals."

"Elephants."

She nodded.

"Why do acrobats make you jealous?"

"Because I couldn't even do a basic cartwheel in school." She tossed her hands up as if the answer was obvious.

"How old is your brother?"

"I'm reminded of that scene in Uncle Buck when Macaulay Culkin grilled John Candy."

Without warning, Rye slung his arm around her shoulders and tugged her in for a kiss. The faded roar of an Aerosmith song combined with the cicadas out here closer to them was the perfect sound for the moment. Chantele cupped his face in her hand, thrilling at the scrape of his dirty blond scruff on her palm.

Inside, she'd been in control. She'd kissed him. Right now, Rye was completely in control, his lips hungry and firm over hers. He tangled his fingers in her hair when she came up for air, giving her only a second before pressing his lips to hers again.

"What was that for?"

"Seemed necessary." He kissed the corner of her mouth. "I'm a middle-aged cowboy not a child star."

"Middle-aged," she repeated with an eye roll.

"Little too old to be making out outside the Iron Stag."

"We're not making out," she reminded him. "You're interviewing me."

Chantele jumped when her phone buzzed in her back pocket. She leaned toward him and slipped it from her pocket.

Get that ride yet?

CHAPTER EIGHT

Rye

"She means me, doesn't she?" Rye squeezed his eyes shut and pinched the bridge of his nose. Of course that text could only be about him. About Chantele hitting on him. Hoping to *ride* him.

"What?" Chantele sounded slightly panicked. Further confirmation that the text on her screen from her friend Nova was about him. And what might be happening out here. Rye opened his eyes and stared absently at the back wall of the Stag, where ironically, he did make out with a girl once. About fifteen years ago.

"Definitely too old to be playing this game." He sighed and climbed off the table.

"Wait." Chantele shook her head. "What? Where are you going?"

"Back inside." Rye took a few steps but stopped when she spoke again.

"You didn't tell me about your long haul."

"*Love*, Chantele." He turned to look at her. "I wanna love someone more than I need my next breath."

She leaned back, propped herself on her hands.

"And I want that woman to love me more than bars and drinks and games."

"I mean, don't we all want that?" she asked softly.

Rye answered with a dramatic shrug. "Do we? You sure as hell never mentioned the word."

"We're in a bar," she reminded him. "Most bar scenes don't involve the *love* word."

"True," he agreed with a nod. "You'd think I'd learn to stay away from the bar scene."

This time, he turned and headed back to the door. Chantele could follow or stay, he didn't care. She would be safe. No one would bother her out here. Rye yanked the door open, and bits of loud conversation and laughter mixed with The Eagles hit him in the face. He had no intention of sticking around any longer. He'd simply go inside and tell Mav he was leaving.

He found Mav head-to-head with Marlowe at the bar. In years past, that could have been trouble brewing. Mav had hit on Marlowe a few times, but she'd friend-zoned him way before even going out with Rye. They were good friends, all of them, which made Rye assume they were now huddled up talking about him. The fact that he'd left the bar with a woman. Probably taking bets on how far things would go out back.

“Headin’ out.” He poked Mav in the shoulder.

“No way.” His friend turned his head, his whole upper body still launched halfway over the bar to be close to Marlowe. “Already?”

“See ya tomorrow.”

“What about—?” Mav spun around now, gaze sweeping Rye, the dance floor, and finally the table where Chantele had been sitting earlier with her friends. “Where’s she at?”

“Outside.”

“Oh.” Mav nodded, the look in his eyes telling Rye exactly what he assumed.

“No.” Rye shook his head and looked past Mav to Marlowe. “Night, Mar.”

To her credit, Marlowe simply nodded.

“Close out my tab on my card?”

She nodded again and turned away from them. Mav made a show of watching the door, his head turning toward the table again. Rye took a quick glance over his shoulder as Chantele returned to the table with her friends.

He might have been into her. If he hadn’t seen that text, he might have spent a little more time with her. More kissing. Touching. For fuck’s sake, he might have taken her home with him. Asked for her number. Something. No question he was attracted to her. And he’d enjoyed the sparring, though he wasn’t sure she would say the same. His questions had irritated her more than anything. Apparently, she was after one thing and his attempts at conversation, at getting to know her, were taking up too much of her time.

Hell, if he didn't like his job, his life, his family, so damned much, maybe it would be time to hit the highway and explore new territory. Not necessarily new women, but new possibilities. Or maybe he should just start going to church and find a woman there. Maybe she wouldn't know how to nose or chew bourbon, but a woman he found at church wouldn't be itching to get in his pants and then dump him, either. Would she?

Fuck if he knew. So much of the buzz in society these days was women's rights and the me-too movement. Hell, he was all for women's rights. He liked powerful women. He admired his mother, his sisters. His mom had raised four kids and worked full time since he could remember. And she didn't just clock in at the Piggly Wiggly and work the checkout lane either. Not that Rye found a damned thing wrong with that. But his mom had gone to nursing school when he was younger. He'd been six or seven, Jolie had been four, and Mom had been pregnant. She'd had Susie just before passing her boards, and then a year into her job at the hospital, she'd been pregnant again with Angie. Four damned little kids running around the house doing what kids do, and his mom had worked her ass off in labor and delivery at the hospital.

Women wanted and deserved respect. Rye was on board. His sister Jolie was an engineer at a company that manufactured farm equipment. She'd been married for two years now, and Rye had overheard her talking to Mom about trying to get pregnant. He'd ducked out of the room on a mission for mind bleach, because as much as he respected women and their right to work and play and raise children and do whatever they pleased, he also didn't want to think about that stuff with his little sister.

The thing that pissed him off? Women complained about being treated as sexual objects. And then turned around and treated men as sexual objects. Seemed like it was a double standard. Seemed like some women were only in favor of tipping the scales, the balance of power, rather than equality.

Chantele had sized him up and decided she wanted to fuck him. Rye's dick liked the idea. He cupped himself and tried to adjust things as he settled into his truck. But he was tired of it. How many damned city girls wandered into the Iron Stag or other downhome taverns looking for cowboys to ride these days? Way too damned many for his liking. Thanks to that damned cowboy show with the men every woman he knew lost their minds over. It would blow over. Probably. First it had been motorcycle guys and gangs. And yes, there were biker bars in the area, too, like the Brown Jug in Kissing Springs. Women lost their shit over professional athletes, too. Now cowboys. He'd just grit his teeth and hold on, wait for the next big thing.

Maybe then he could find a woman interested in something more than a romp.

He might just be in his mid-thirties, but if he looked hard enough, he could see forty coming. His parents had been married—hell, they'd had him and Jolie before they were thirty. At the rate Rye was going, if he ever had kids, he'd be one of those gray-haired dads people mistakenly assumed was a kid's grandpa instead of a dad.

He started the truck and dropped it into gear. The Iron Stag grew smaller in the rearview mirror as he pulled out on the two-lane highway. Maybe it was time to quit the Stag, focus on a different lifestyle, and get away from the buckle bunnies.

CHAPTER NINE

Chantele

Chantele sipped from her coffee as she read the list of ingredients in the French toast casserole. Brown sugar. Eggs. Milk. Vanilla. Cinnamon. She tapped the print button on her laptop as her stomach rumbled.

"Not for you," she muttered and rubbed her free hand over her belly.

She'd lost the bet. How in the hell had that happened? She wasn't a bombshell, but how in the hell in this day and age did a woman walk into a bar hoping to hook up with a cowboy and walk out empty-handed?

Well. She supposed she could have won the bet easily enough if she'd made a play for Maverick instead of Rye. Maybe that said there was *something* worth saving about her—she might have wanted a hook-up with a cowboy, but she had standards. She'd zeroed in on the guy she wanted, and he'd walked away from her.

And now she was stocking up on breakfast recipes. Her plan was a bit devious. She would start with yummy, fattening dishes for her two best friends. They would gripe good-naturedly about the sugar and the calories, but Chantele knew they would gobble the goodies down. When they finally started anticipating her treats, she would switch tactics and start bringing them healthy things like oatmeal or scrambled egg whites.

Better yet, protein shakes. With kale.

She snickered as she put her coffee down and rolled her chair back. Time to get busy. She'd grab the recipe off the printer and get down to business.

And stop thinking about the bet she lost.

After all, the trip was supposed to be for Paisley. And that part had been a success. The three of them had spent all day Saturday wandering in and out of the boutiques in Kissing Springs. They'd grabbed lunch at the diner, dinner at the trendy restaurant, Two Fourteen, and then they'd gone for drinks at the Bourbon Boot Scoot. From there, they had managed to score tickets to the male-revue at the Boyd Theater. The guys—apparently, they had started out as stripping Santas—had been super sexy and fun to watch, but after crashing and burning the night before at the Iron Stag, Chantele had accepted defeat on the bet and found herself just as interested in the renovations that had been done to the theater as she was the strippers. She'd been to Kissing Springs once before with Johnny. She had no idea if the male-revue was a thing then. She kind of doubted it, but then she still found it a little surprising there was a male-strip club this side of the Bible Belt at all. She and Johnny had walked the square, so they'd passed the theater, of course. But she didn't recall anything too spectacular about it.

Chantele had come home with a bottle of Lockland Five Year—part of her regretted the purchase the second her card had been approved but part of her had wanted that little piece of Rye when she left. Paisley had bought a few things for the baby, although she refused to buy too much too early, and Nova, being Nova, had found the perfect outfit for the baby's baptism. Chantele and Paisley had gone along with her on that, even knowing that she would wear the flowy, floral-patterned slacks and chartreuse blouse well before the baby was born, let alone baptized, and she would purchase another five or six outfits for the baptism between now and then.

Printed recipe in hand, Chantele sat down again, folded the recipe over and tucked it in her desk calendar to take home later. She would hit the grocery store on the way home and get everything she would need for her first breakfast weekend. Her phone buzzed as she tapped her keyboard. She ignored it, intending to focus on a campaign for a new local client. Jewel Tones would open in two weeks; Chantele was working on a blow-out grand opening for them.

She'd been working with a colleague on the graphics for the ad, so Chantele opened her file to tweak the marketing pitch. Her phone blew up with five or six rapid notifications. With a groan, she took her fingers from the keyboard, rested her hands on the desk, and gave the phone a dirty look. Apparently, it wasn't scared of her because it buzzed again.

While she doubted there was an emergency, it was always possible her parents needed something. Or even her brother or sister-in-law. Resolving to see what the excitement was and then put her phone away and get to work, Chantele picked her phone up and held her breath as she looked at the screen.

Three texts. None from family. No emergencies.

Except for the text from Nova claiming an emergency.

WTF?

Right? Touchy much?

Scroll on by, dude.

With a weary sigh, Chantele flopped back in her chair and tapped out a quick response.

What's going on?

Have u seen ur ig?

"My Instagram?" Chantele mumbled with a frown. Well, no, she hadn't looked at it since last night when she'd posted pictures from their girls' weekend. She assumed Nova and Paisley had done the same, so what was the big to-do about her page? Rather than answer Nova and Paisley, she tapped out of the text thread and opened Instagram.

Several mutual friends had liked the pictures. Her sister-in-law left a comment—*looks like the perfect getaway.* There were a few other comments, including one from someone at Two Fourteen, thanking them for their visit and encouraging them to leave a review for the restaurant.

Her heart skipped a beat when she saw the screen name MavMan. Well, no mystery who that was.

Smokin' hot ladies. Come see Bogart again soon.

Okay, so she didn't love that Maverick had found her—she had to assume Nova and Mav had exchanged numbers and maybe other things—but that comment wasn't a big deal. She scrolled on and held her breath when the next screen name hit her. GRye.

His comment seemed to be in response not to the pictures she'd posted, but her caption and hashtags.

#girlsweekend #cowboys #mechanicalbull #whenyouloseabet #suckitup #breakfastduty #justkeeplooking

GRye clearly took offense to the bet.

Then again, why would that surprise her? Wasn't that why he'd clammed up and stormed off at the bar over the weekend?

Nice.

One word. And yet, that one word knocked the wind out of her. Guilt settled, souring the coffee on her empty stomach.

Anyone who hadn't been there probably thought GRye's comment was sincere. Like he thought it was nice they had a good girls' weekend. Her best friends read it as the passive aggressive comment it was because she'd filled them in on what had happened.

But as Chantele stared at that one word on her screen, shame flooded her. Dammit. If she reversed the roles here and she had seen a post he shared with a hashtag about a bet, after what had happened at the bar—or worse, after what didn't happen at the bar—she would be hurt. Pissed off. And probably a lot meaner than leaving a one-word passive aggressive comment.

She couldn't respond to him on Instagram. She liked to share pictures with friends and family, but she wasn't one to air dirty laundry in public. But she did owe him an apology. They hadn't exchanged numbers, so she would either have to send him a private message on the forum or ask Nova to get his number from Maverick.

That was unacceptable. Childish. As their bet had been. Chantele hadn't given much thought to what a cowboy would think about her attempt to seduce him into a one-night stand. But on this side of the ordeal, she realized it wasn't exactly in good taste. She wouldn't make it worse by dragging her friends and Mav along for her apology. She would just send him a private message on Instagram.

CHAPTER TEN

Rye

Rye tossed his hat on the passenger seat where Jax Connors had been sitting just a minute ago. Robert had sent the two of them out to the south pasture to check the fences. Rye didn't mind, but Jax ran his damned mouth the way Derby horses ran the track—fast and furious. The last forty-five minutes of his day had worn him out more than the other ten hours put together.

He put the truck in park and killed the ignition, doing his best to shove away everything Jax had just shared with him. No, Rye wasn't getting any action—not that he would tell Jax that—and yes, he had done a hell of a lot of thinking about Chantele after that night at the Iron Stag. But that didn't make him desperate enough to want to listen to some damned wet-behind-the-ears cowboy relive his night out on the town last weekend.

Jax had already disappeared inside the barn by the time Rye climbed out of his truck. He supposed that was about his youth, too. The problem with that—with Jax and the other young guys Robert Pressey had hired recently—was that Rye hadn't felt that old before they'd all shown up. But with all the old aches and pains from the hard, outdoor work, from the hours in the saddle, from life—he'd broken his ankle playing basketball his freshman year of college—watching these young guys move like they greased their joints with magic juice had almost been an insult.

Couple that with his run-in with Chantele, with the hard-on he'd had for her since that weekend, and seeing her Instagram post, and Rye felt ancient. He only had an account on that app because of his sisters. Wasn't like he had time to deal with any of that crap.

And then damned Mav had to go and tell him to look at Chantele's pictures. One peek had set him off again. She was pretty *and* cute, and he'd tried to explain that to Mav, but near as he could tell, Mav wasn't getting what he meant. Or if he was, he was just being stubborn. The pictures on Chantele's page showed her and her friends enjoying Kissing Springs, and naturally, they'd gone to the Boyd Theater to take in the male-revue. Rye hadn't had too much time wonder about that, to wonder if Chantele had found some other cowboy to give her a ride, before he'd glanced at her captions and hashtags. He'd seen the word *bet*. And then he'd seen red. No idea what the details of the bet were, but Rye was two hundred percent certain they involved Chantele getting naked with a cowboy.

Could've been him.

Maverick had sure ribbed him about it enough in the days since.

Rye didn't regret turning her down so much as he did learning she was at the Iron Stag solely for a hookup. They'd clashed; no question they might burn down a room if they spent any time together, and not in any fun kind of way.

But she was interesting.

Sexy.

Fuck yes, she was hot, and he'd spent the last several nights thinking about her.

He'd commented on her post. Mostly because he couldn't help himself, because he was angry. Wasn't like he would ever see her again. Or hear from her. They hadn't swapped much besides a little bit of spit and first names.

Mav, on the other hand, had apparently exchanged numbers with Nova, and he'd started following her on social media and vice versa. How the hell Maverick found the time or energy to care enough to look at social media, let alone post anything, Rye had no idea.

He found Robert in the corral behind the barn. His boss ran a brush over the shiny black shoulder of his mount, murmuring to him as if he didn't know Rye had approached. Rye knew better. Robert Pressey had more and better senses than Spiderman.

"Fences look good," Rye announced.

If Rye hadn't been watching closely, he would have missed Robert's slight nod.

"I need you and Jax and Mav on that shed tomorrow."

Building a shed was fine. Rye enjoyed swinging a hammer and using a saw. He liked the smell of sawdust and fresh cut wood as much as he liked the smell of rawhide and leather. And the fact that Robert was adding a building to the ranch —whether it be a new shed for storage, another barn for the horses, or an addition to the house he shared with Charlene Pressey—added up to a good sign. The Pressey ranch was holding its own even with the national economy grinding its gears and slowing down.

But damned if Rye wanted to be saddled with Jax again. Not that he'd complain. He'd done his share of that bullshit when he was in high school, griping about this teammate or that teammate, frustrated with his lab partner or group projects, and what he'd learned was life wasn't fair. You played the hand you're dealt. Jax was a pain in his ass; hell, Mav was a pain in his ass. But nothing he couldn't handle. And damned sure nothing he'd take to his boss.

He snagged a bottle of water on the way back through the barn. Mav reclined in the chair, booted feet up on Robert's desk. Rye only tapped his knuckles on the desk, drawing Mav's gaze. His buddy was on the office phone, probably tracking down a missing feed order or talking to Dr. Kooley about the pregnant mare due to give birth within the next few weeks.

Mav mouthed something to him, but Rye had no idea what he was trying to say and no desire to linger and find out it was something about Nova or Chantele. Just his luck—he'd like to be rid of that memory forever and Mav had gone rogue and befriended one of them.

Hell. Who knew? Maybe Mav had done more than befriend Nova. Rye didn't care to ask, and thankfully, Mav didn't share stories like he used to when they were younger. When Rye gave him a quick salute, Mav simply nodded and rolled his eyes. Listening to someone talk nonstop, Rye decided, as he headed back out to his truck.

He tipped the water bottle up for a drink as he climbed up in the driver's seat and started the truck. Warm wind whipped through his open windows as he headed down the long, paved drive and made a right onto the highway. He rolled his head around on his neck and caught his eye in the rearview mirror. The prerequisite hat ring circled his head; sweat dampened his hairline. The scruff on his face was getting a little out of hand. He'd have to trim it up a bit tonight after a cool shower and a cold beer.

While he enjoyed his cold beer, he would throw a big pork chop on the grill and eat a handful of spinach and call it a salad. One benefit of living alone, he told himself. Although getting to eat whatever he wanted didn't really balance out the fact that he was tired of sleeping alone.

CHAPTER ELEVEN

Chantele

Still nothing.

She was being stupid. Her brain knew it. But something inside her wouldn't let it go. Four days had passed since she'd apologized to Rye via private message on Instagram, and he hadn't said a damned word.

Chantele knew it was better left alone, but she knew herself well enough to know she'd poke the bear until he snapped. In fact, she'd messaged him again on the app earlier this morning, as she was leaving her apartment for work. When he hadn't responded by the time she grabbed lunch, she found herself stabbing bites of romaine and spinach with the force necessary to spear fish. Being the professional she was, she shoved Rye to the back burner in her brain for the rest of the afternoon. But being the childish brat she was apparently determined to be, she called Nova on her drive home, so she could get in touch with Rye. Either through

Nova and Mav or getting Mav's number from Nova and texting him.

Unfortunately, Nova didn't answer her call. Chantele had groaned out loud when voicemail picked up, but she calmed herself before leaving a message and simply asked Nova for Maverick's number.

Her heels clicked across the parking garage as she made her way to the door. She'd dropped her phone in her purse figuring Nova wouldn't respond for a while. If nothing else, Chantele would call her again later, after she found something for dinner.

She wouldn't admit to Nova or Paisley that she wondered about calling Rye through Instagram. She didn't spend much time on social media, but she knew there were some apps you could use to make phone calls. She'd done so a time or two, accidentally, and struggled to end the call before anyone could pick up. In the end, she hadn't checked to see if she could do it on Instagram.

Now, she tapped her key card to the magnetic lock on the main door of the complex and tugged the door open. Running through a mental list of her refrigerator contents for dinner ideas, she pushed the elevator button and then checked her mailbox. She withdrew the few envelopes there, noting two were junk mail and one a bill. She turned her nose up and dashed into the elevator when the doors opened.

She should just let it go. That would be the adult thing to do. But the fact that he'd dumped her—well, sort of—he'd kissed her and then he'd just dropped her and left her alone outside the Iron Stag rubbed her the wrong way. And then for him to comment on her post? If he'd only done it to goad her into a response, it worked. Even if it was just to get under her skin.

The elevator stopped at her floor; Chantele strode off, head turned to the right to catch a glimpse of the day out the floor-to-ceiling windows in the small hallway. Much too beautiful to be inside wallowing in indignation over being passed over by that damned cowboy.

Mind made up, she made her way down the corridor to her apartment and let herself in. She tossed her key and purse on the counter and went directly to the refrigerator for water. Change clothes. Find something for dinner, even if it was a simple grilled cheese sandwich, and then get outside for a walk.

And forget the whole damned bet and Rye and the kiss.

Kisses.

Truth be told, that's what really stung. The kisses were hot. And sweet. She'd spent way too much time remembering the feel of his lips on hers, the press of his thighs against hers, the taste of the beer on his tongue.

She chugged a long swallow of water, put the bottle on the counter, and then hurried to her bedroom, stripping off her work clothes as she went. She didn't throw them on the floor, simply carried them to her room and dropped them in the hamper. Bike shorts and an oversized t-shirt later, she returned to the kitchen and found a bell pepper, an onion, and a few suspicious-looking mushrooms in the refrigerator. Double-checking to make sure she had brown rice, she decided a quick veggie stir-fry sounded good.

Her phone buzzed as she squatted to grab a skillet from the cabinet. She stilled, crouched in front of the cabinet, and then made herself move. She would get her dinner going and then see if that text was from Nova. She could be an adult about this.

Skillet on the burner, she took the cutting board from a different cabinet, selected a knife, and started slicing the vegetables. She'd turn on music, but that would involve getting her phone from her purse. And she refused do that because she would crack and look at her texts and then she'd fall right back down the petulant anger hole. The stupid need to have the last word would eat away at her, and she would forget to eat until it was late, and she was ready for bed.

With the veggies sliced and heating in a splash of avocado oil in the skillet, Chantele poured a cup of rice and a cup of water in a saucepan and turned that burner on, too. She reached for her phone, but slowed, eyes on the small wine rack on the counter. A glass of chardonnay sounded good. But would she feel like taking a walk if she had wine now?

What if she ate dinner, took a walk, and then had a glass of wine? She could read for a while before she went to bed.

"God, Chan," she groaned out loud, nearly jumping at the sound of her own voice in the empty kitchen. "What a freaking exciting life you live."

The most thrilling thing to happen to her lately was kissing that cowboy. Rye. And sparring with him. He'd kind of rubbed her the wrong way that night at the bar, but based on how he kissed, Chantele guessed he could probably rub her the right way, too.

No wonder she wanted to poke back at him. It was something out of the ordinary. Chantele loved her job. Her friends. And even though she would gripe come Saturday morning when it was time to get up and fix breakfast and then deliver breakfast to her friends, she didn't really mind that. It was how she and her friends rolled, and it wouldn't be long before there was another bet in place.

But Chantele couldn't deny she had hoped for a fling when she was in Rodey or Kissing Springs. And once she'd laid eyes on that cowboy, she'd hoped for a fling with him. Once she'd started talking to him, she'd hoped they would do that fling and exchange numbers.

Interacting with him now, the apology and the poke she intended to deliver if she could get his phone number, wasn't what she'd planned. But it was better than nothing.

Decision made—wine later—she reached into her purse and found her phone.

Got a dinner meeting. R u really gonna call him?

Nova had shared Maverick's contact information.

One step closer. Chantele put her phone down to check the vegetables. She would text Mav and simply ask for Rye's number. No need for explanations. If Mav didn't give it to her, then she'd be at a dead end, and maybe she'd be ready to let it go then.

Doubtful, but possible.

CHAPTER TWELVE

Rye

“What the fuck are you doing?” Mav snapped. On his knees at the end of the two by four, he watched Rye pat down his pocket with a sigh.

“Damn phone’s ringing,” he grunted with frustration as he picked up the lumber and carried it closer to Mav. Rye held the two by four in place as Mav hammered the two together. They’d framed two of the walls so far. It wasn’t hard work, by any means, at least not this part. But Rye was grumpy, and the damned phone ringing in his pocket did nothing to make that better.

“Probably a call about your truck warranty,” Mav mumbled, head still tipped as he studied the nails he’d just driven into the wood. With a nod, he scooted down the board and looked up as Rye carried another two by four over to him.

Rye snorted and rolled his eyes.

“Just turned over 73,” he told Mav.

"What year is it?"

"'Nineteen," he answered. "Pretty sure I didn't purchase a warranty on it."

Mav shrugged as he lined up the lumber and whacked the nail with the hammer. "Pretty sure that doesn't matter to those people."

"One more," Rye announced as he grabbed the final two by four for this wall and brought it to Mav. Robert had pulled Jax from the shed project after they'd framed the first wall. Jax was now working with Rodney to clean up storm damage in one of the north pastures. The winds last night had taken several heavy limbs down. Rye hadn't slept well; he'd started out stewing over the strawberry blonde that wouldn't get out of his head and then as the storm kicked up, he'd worried about the horses. Robert would see to them, Rye knew that. And if things had gotten too bad, Rye would've have dressed and headed to the ranch at two rather than his usual four a.m.

His phone buzzed in his pocket again. Not used to the barrage of messages, he almost jumped. Mav cut him a questioning glance at his long-suffering sigh.

"What the hell's with you?"

"Phone just buzzed again." Rye rolled his eyes.

"Message about your car." Mav nodded.

"Probably one of my sisters asking a favor."

"The worst," Mav agreed. He peeked at Rye but quickly ducked his head again. Rye had made it clear Mav was never to joke about or flirt with any of his sisters. And when

Mav had broken that rule and kissed Jolie after her graduation, Rye had given him a black eye. And now, usually, Mav pretended Rye didn't have any siblings.

"Jesus." Rye snapped and pulled his phone from his pocket as he straightened.

"More?"

He ignored Mav's question and stared at his phone as it buzzed again in his hand. There was a voicemail from an unknown number. And an unread text message. Rye took a quick look around as he tapped the voicemail icon and put the phone to his ear.

"Don't hang up."

He wasn't sure if it was her voice or what she'd said, but he hung up.

"Spam?" Mav asked, finally standing. He swept his gaze over the wall they'd just framed. "We need Jax to give us a hand to get these raised."

"How the hell did she get my number?"

"What?" Mav shot him a look over his shoulder as he moved to the other end of the wall.

"Need a hand?" Robert called.

Rye shoved his phone in his pocket as Robert approached them. Dressed in his worn boots and faded Wranglers, no one would look at him and assume he was the landowner here. He fit right in, both in appearance and work ethic.

"That'd be good." Mav nodded in appreciation at his father. "Ready to stand these up."

The three of them worked as a team—Rye and Mav holding two skeletal walls up as Robert drilled screws into the wood to hold them together and then drilled each of the walls into the wooden skid flooring.

"Who's she?" Mav finally asked him.

"Shit." Rye groaned. "You did it, didn't you?"

"Did what?"

"Did you give that woman my number?"

"Chantele?" Mav grinned. "I thought you'd want to talk to her."

"Woman trouble?" Robert asked, clearly amused by their conversation.

"No. What I have is a problem with your asshole son," Rye told him, no venom in his words.

"Who is she?"

"Girl from Lexington," Mav told Robert.

Rye shot him a look meant to shut him up. No need to discuss Chantele at all, most definitely not in front of Robert.

"City girl." Robert nodded.

"She made a play for our boy at the Iron Stag."

"Shut up, Mav."

"Yeah?" Robert quirked an eyebrow at Rye. "Still talking to her, huh?"

Rye chose not to correct his boss on what had and hadn't happened at the tavern. The quicker he killed this conversation, the better.

"Charlene came onto me," Robert reminded Mav and Rye. Even wishing he could erase the conversation, Mav's groan at Robert's words made Rye's lips twitch with a smile. "Sometimes those little hellcat women are loads of fun."

"Uncle." Mav shook his head. "Stop."

"Only sometimes?" Rye egged Robert on.

"Well." The older man grinned. "Guess they're always fun, but you never know what kinda fun each day's gonna bring."

"And I'm done." Mav dropped his hands and turned away from the walls. "Lemme just go find some bleach. Maybe if I snort it, it'll clean my brain out."

"You got room to talk, boy." Robert propped a screw between his teeth and concentrated on the wooden frame again. Rye watched him take the screw and set it for the drill. "You know how many damned times your mother caught you makin' out with girls? Damned woman was scared to death you'd get some girl pregnant before you got outta high school. Now here we are, twenty years later, and still not one damned grandbaby."

"Twenty's a bit on the high end, Dad," Mav argued.

"It's a number, son," Robert mumbled. "The point being as randy as you are, you're never gonna settle down and give your mother and me a grandchild."

"Randy?" Mav mouthed the word at Rye.

"He's got a point." Rye shrugged.

Robert nodded and pointed at Rye in agreement.

"Fucker." Mav rolled his eyes.

"Payback, fucker." Rye grinned.

"Alright." Robert backed up and eyed the structure of the shed for a moment. Three-sided, skeletal, and no roof. They were killing it today. The damned thing should have been standing an hour ago, and Rye knew it. "You get this finished today. Need you to run some horses this afternoon. Stryker and Beau need some exercise."

CHAPTER THIRTEEN

Chantele

"What?"

Chantele pulled her phone from her ear and narrowed her eyes at it.

"Are you kidding me? That's how you answer phone calls?" She let herself into her apartment and tossed her purse and keys on the counter. "Maybe that's why you don't get laid."

"Who says I don't get laid?"

"You did. You stormed off that night because you were mad. Because you're looking for love."

The cowboy had the nerve to sigh. Not just a regular sigh, but one heavy with frustration. She could almost hear him counting to ten, like he was trying not to lose his temper with her.

"There's a difference in getting laid and finding love, Chantele," he answered, voice clipped and stern, like he'd put a cork in his anger to hold it back. "Precisely the point I made at the Iron Stag when I *walked* away from you. I did not *storm* off."

"Same difference."

"Agree to disagree," he answered. "What do you want?"

"Really?" She put her phone, screen up, on the counter and stared at it with a frown. "Did you not see Instagram?"

"As a matter of fact, I did."

She flinched at the sharp note in his tone again.

"I saw pictures of three beautiful women who appeared to have had a nice girls' weekend in Kissing Springs and the surrounding area. And I saw hashtags referencing a lost bet."

Chantele dragged her teeth over her lip and drew in a breath so deep her nostrils flared. So, he'd seen the pictures and the hashtags but not her apology. That made his testiness with her on the phone a bit easier to swallow, but on the other hand, why the hell had he taken the time to look at the pictures and get pissed about the hashtags and then never look again to see her apology?

"And because I'm not some uneducated cowpoke, I'm going to assume the lost bet had something to do with the text on your phone about getting a ride."

"Rye." She cleared her throat and took a deep breath, but apparently, he wasn't done talking.

"I don't know. Maybe you think I was supposed to be flattered. But it—"

"I'm sorry."

"What?"

"I'm sorry," she repeated. "I'm only calling because I sent you an apology through private messages on the app, and I didn't hear back from you."

"You sent an apology?"

"Yes."

"For what?"

Chantele closed her eyes and dropped her head back. Afraid her extreme frustration would come out as a screech of rage, she clamped her teeth together and counted to three.

"Because yes, you're right. My friends and I have always made a game of crazy dares and bets, and yes, they bet me I couldn't sleep with a cowboy before the weekend was over. And yes, I was hoping to...use you...to win the bet."

The silence stretched long enough that Chantele wondered if he'd ended the call.

"How much did you lose?"

Chantele snorted softly and leaned over to rest her elbows on the counter on opposite sides of her phone. She eased out of her heels and closed her eyes in pleasure when her feet met the cool tile floor.

"I have to make breakfast for them every weekend for the next six months."

"Damn." He groaned softly. "You shoulda just said so. Maybe I'd have helped you out."

The laugh escaped her before she decided it was funny.

"Okay." She sighed. "So. Sorry to bother you—"

"Who gave you my number?"

"Mav. Nova hooked me up with him. I just wanted to make sure you got my apology. Because. Yeah. You're right. The bet was kind of shitty, and if the tables had been turned, I would be upset, too."

Again, Chantele's words were met with silence. Wondering again if he'd ended the call or if he was angry, she rambled.

"I have to say I didn't expect to get turned down. I know I'm not a sex kitten, and I'm not even the seductress Nova is, but it was a *bar*. A tavern in the middle of nowhere. Never—"

"You are every bit the sex kitten you wanted to be that night, Chantele," he corrected her. "You're still living rent free in my head. You just marked the wrong guy. I'm too old for more games. If you had hit on Mav, you wouldn't be slogging cereal to your friends every weekend for the next six months."

"Well." She took a deep breath and straightened at the counter. "I didn't want Mav. Still wouldn't. I'll deal with the breakfast duty. At least I got a couple of kisses out of you."

He was quiet again, but Chantele heard faint voices in the background, so she knew the call was still going.

"Goodnight, Rye."

"Night."

She tapped the screen to end the call and then stared at her phone a moment longer. Okay, she felt better for the phone call. Apologizing to him—sincerely. Wasn't quite the same as face to face, but better than a typed message, she supposed.

Too bad that had gone so horribly wrong from the word go. Despite the way they'd sparred, hell, maybe *because* of the way they'd sparred, Chantele wished they could talk more. See each other again.

She turned away, intending to change from her office clothes to workout clothes. A walk wouldn't contain this wired feeling she had now. Nope. She would head to the gym and do a little cardio and some weight training.

Her phone buzzed as she left the kitchen.

After a slight hesitation, she turned and walked back to the counter. Her heart thudded up her throat when she saw the text.

Did you mean that?

Rye.

She hadn't put a last name in her phone. Simply Rye, so she could make sure to contact him and say she was sorry and then delete it.

Did I mean what?

Her fingers tingled with nervous energy as she held her phone and watched the three dots appear and then vanish. Over and over again. Was he toying with her? Was that the game? She deserved it, but she didn't like it.

That you didn't want Mav.

You said it, Rye. If I had wanted Mav, I could have had him.

She put her phone down again and took two steps away before turning back again.

I didn't. I'd much rather fry bacon until next fall than have slept with Mav just to win a bet.

CHAPTER FOURTEEN

Rye

So, what's for breakfast this weekend?

Rye huffed out a sigh as he tossed his phone on the bed. He had told himself he wouldn't do this. Yes, he had Chantele's number, but all he had to do was ignore it. Or better yet, delete it. Delete the call she had made. And walk away.

But he'd been thinking about her before she'd swallowed her pride and called him to apologize. Before she'd reiterated that she wasn't interested in Maverick. The one guy every woman in bourbon country wanted to do or claim.

How the hell was he supposed to just let it go now? He had managed to wait a day before texting her, although he'd been thinking all day about what to say to her. He wouldn't question her again about Mav. For one thing, he wasn't desperate. Interested, yes. Desperate, no. Did he feel inferior to Mav? No. He'd asked; she'd answered. End of that story.

But he climbed out of bed before dawn and dressed and grabbed his thermos of coffee this morning, and the minute he'd put his damned hat on, he'd thought of her again. All morning while he had fed the horses and mucked the stalls and bullshitted here and there with Mav and Jax and the other guys—even Robert—he'd thought about Chantele and what to say to her to continue the conversation.

It was late in the afternoon, after he and Mav had finished the walls of the shed and Rye took Fleet out for a run, that he decided he would just start a new one. No need to revisit the weekend—the bet, the bull, none of that mattered.

He had dropped in at the Iron Stag when he left the ranch, but he only had one beer. Marlowe had been tied up with a rowdy bunch of city guys; Rye assumed it was a bachelor party or something. He had nursed his beer long enough to see that his friend was completely at ease with the group, and then he left before Maverick could show up and buy a round. Rye had reheated the leftover plate his mom had delivered, put his feet up on his postage stamp-sized patio while he ate, and sipped a beer. Once that was done, once he had thought his fill of Chantele outside, picturing her here in his territory, in his little house, he had gone inside and cleaned up his small mess in the kitchen and watched a couple of episodes of *House of the Dragon*. He'd tried to do the cowboy shows—*Longmire* and *Yellowstone*—but he lived that life. Minus the murders and most of the drug issues Longmire dealt with. Rye was more the *Game of Thrones* fantasy type than a cowboy fan.

His phone buzzed. Even though his heartbeat snapped to attention, he took his time reaching for the phone to see if the message was from Chantele.

French toast casserole.

The fuck is French toast casserole and where can I get some?

French toast. In a casserole. Your address is out of my delivery zone.

Damn. That sounds good.

If you'd have slept with me, I could be making it for you this weekend, instead of these two.

The laugh that rolled up from his gut surprised him.

I have regrets.

That ship's sailed.

He laughed again, even though he did feel a twitch of regret. He was glad he hadn't taken her home that night, because even if he had, she would have gone back to Lexington, and they wouldn't be texting. It would have been a fling, mutually enjoyable, he assumed, but nothing more would come of it. But he wished now there could have been more.

With a sigh, he told her goodnight, put his phone on the charger, and turned his light off. Lexington wasn't that far away, but it wasn't Rodey, either. He couldn't hop in his truck and head that way and knock on doors until he found her. The thought brought a smile to his face as he lay there in the dark imagining going door to door with a ladies' cowboy hat or boot, looking for Chantele like she was his Cinderella.

That was the problem, though. He was never going to be anyone's Prince Charming.

Up before dawn again, he was well-rested. But before he even walked out of his house, he was thinking about her. He was going to text her again; he knew it just the same as he knew it wasn't a good idea. Just the same as he had known in tenth grade that taking a swing at senior Jeb Browning wasn't a good idea.

He wouldn't end up with a black eye and bruised ribs if he texted Chantele again, but he might end up with a broken heart.

"Dramatic, much?" He snorted to himself as he climbed into his truck, thermos of coffee in hand, and pulled the door closed behind him. Okay, he was nowhere near broken heart territory. If she blew him off, it wouldn't be the end of the world. And who knew? Maybe she would make him laugh again.

CHAPTER FIFTEEN

CHANTELE

If Chantele had been surprised when Rye texted to ask her what was for breakfast that first weekend after she lost the bet, she was floored when they were still texting a month later. At first, she'd let him start the conversation or pick back up on the thread when things got quiet. After all, he'd turned her down. Intellectually, she understood that making a bet with her friends and attempting to use him to win the bet was wrong. But there was still a sliver of woman inside her that stung from the brush off.

He always asked about the breakfasts she was planning. Chantele had taken to sending him pictures. Sometimes she sent screenshots of recipes. Sometimes she sent him a shot of her grocery cart. Once, she sent him a selfie when she was fixing an omelet in Nova's kitchen. Rye always had some snide, fun comment. When she sent the selfie, he answered with a GIF of a cartoon cat with its eyes bugging out. Ignoring the little thrill that created in her belly, Chantele had sent him the eye roll emoji in return.

They progressed to discussions about things other than breakfast. Chantele asked him what he did for a living. She hadn't believed him at first when he sent her a picture of a horse barn.

What? U think I'm just a pretend cowboy?

That text had made her laugh, but she eventually admitted that yes, she just assumed he dressed that way and worked at a factory or something. Which was the perfect opportunity for him to send her the eye roll emoji.

He sent pictures of horses. A picture of Mav atop a horse. Chantele sent another eye roll in response. She was intrigued to learn that Mav's father owned a lot of horses, that Rye worked on Mav's father's horse ranch. They talked about their families. Swapped jokes and memes. And Chantele found herself wishing things would have been different. That they'd started different.

Sure, he'd been a little prickly at the bar. Well, she had, too, she guessed. But that whole thing where he thought he'd summed her up with his guess that she worked in sales and wanted marriage and a townhouse and bougie coffee—that had set her off. When she thought about it, which was often, she got it. He probably already had her figured out by then, and he was probably offended or angry or both, and he'd gone on the offensive. God knows, she hadn't behaved well.

If they'd hooked up, would they be talking now? Probably not. After all, she'd gone into that weekend looking for sex, not a relationship. And as much as she had wanted him, as much as she wished now that she'd stolen more than a few kisses, Chantele liked that they were talking. Okay, mostly texting. There'd been a few very short phone calls, mostly when one of them needed to actually laugh at the other, to make sure they heard it, to rub in the teasing exchanged.

She liked him. She wished now she could go back and redo how they met, because she wondered if there could have been more for them than what they'd ended up with.

"How's the mama?" Nova asked Paisley.

Chantele hadn't told her friends how often she and Rye talked now. Both knew she'd called and apologized about the bet. Paisley had given her approval, but Nova had rolled her eyes and suggested Rye grow some balls. Both friends knew they'd texted, that Rye had asked that first weekend what she fixed them for breakfast. But she didn't tell them they were still texting. That they did talk on the phone now and then.

There was no reason to hide. But Chantele didn't think there was a reason to make a big deal of it, either. Maybe she considered him a friend now, so it was no different than any of them texting with other friends.

"Hungry." Paisley took a drink of her orange juice and glanced at Chantele. Nova sniffed the air and glanced at the oven.

"What's for breakfast today?"

"Garlic and herb biscuit egg sandwiches," Chantele answered. She leaned on Paisley's counter at her back and slipped her phone from her pocket when it buzzed.

"Holy Mother of God, that sounds delicious." Nova nodded her approval. "And you whipped these biscuits up from scratch?"

"Did the batter last night," Chantele told her, eyes on her phone. She tapped the same answer about today's breakfast to Rye.

"I know what you're doing," Nova announced as she slid into the chair beside Paisley.

"What am I doing?" Chantele asked quickly, willing herself not to drop her phone. If she did that, both of them would be suspicious, and then she'd have to answer a hundred questions about Rye, and as much fun as that *could* be, it wouldn't be. Because there was nothing going on.

"Serving us delicious food to make us fat."

She laughed.

"She's gonna make us dependent on her." Paisley rested her elbows on the table and narrowed her eyes at Chantele. "Like when our six months is up, we'll be at her door every weekend, begging for food like dogs."

"Wow." Chantele rolled her eyes. "Little dramatic, even for you, Pais."

"Smells good." Nova nodded. "Where do you find these recipes?"

"There's this thing called the internet." Chantele put her phone on the counter and turned to grab a cup. "Heard of it?" She filled the cup with coffee and handed it to Nova.

"Smartass." Nova grinned.

"Seriously." Chantele nudged Paisley's shoulder. "How are you?"

"Good," she said simply. "I think I'm out of that initial phase where I'm so tired I can't move."

"Do you know what you're having yet?"

"No."

Chantele opened the oven door to check the biscuits. With five minutes left on the timer, she got the eggs from the refrigerator. Her phone buzzed again.

"But, Pais," Nova argued. "We wanna know."

"Vince and I don't want to know."

Chantele checked her phone. The argument about the baby's sex was one they had every time they saw each other. Nova's playful argument was based on needing to be a good "auntie" for the baby, wanting to have the right colors of onesies and blankets and such for newborn gifts. Paisley and Vince simply wanted to be surprised.

I want to see a picture.

Chantele felt the smirk on her face as she typed her response. *They're not done yet.*

A picture of you. Something cute. An apron. Flour on your nose.

She laughed softly, shook her head, and turned her attention to breakfast again.

"What're you laughing about?" Paisley asked her as she set a skillet on the stove.

"Nothing."

"What about the heartbeat?" Nova asked Paisley.

"Yes. We've heard the heartbeat."

"And was it slow or fast?"

Chantele snorted at Nova still trying to fish an answer out of Paisley about the baby's sex.

I can't take a picture now. Cooking.

Takes two seconds.

Nova and Paisley r right here. Can't with them around.

This time her phone lit up with an incoming call.

Chantele, egg in hand, picked it up and tucked it between her ear and shoulder.

"What?"

"Not that kind of picture."

She barked a laugh, glad her back was to her friends, because an embarrassed heat rushed her face.

"Although I'm good with that, too, if you're up for it."

"Nope." She laughed quietly. "Too late for that."

"Why can't you take a picture if they're there?"

When she didn't answer right away, he asked another question.

"Really? They put you up to propositioning me for sex, but now they don't know that we talk all the time?"

"I didn't proposition you!" she yelped, laughing and spinning around to see her two best friends watching her with wide eyes. "I hit on you."

"You tried to seduce me with that sexy ride you took on Bogart," he reminded her.

"Ouch." She groaned and turned her back to the girls again. "Don't remind me."

"You said it didn't hurt."

"That wasn't the only time I crashed and burned that night."

"Aggressive driving," he mumbled.

"I gotta go. I need to finish breakfast."

"Come and see me."

"Excuse me?"

"Ask your friends for a weekend off and come back to Rodey."

Chantele looked over her shoulder. When she found Nova and Paisley still watching her with big eyes, she wondered if they could hear Rye's side of the conversation, too.

"For what?"

"I'll teach you how to ride that bull without falling off."

"The only reason I got on that damned thing was to get your attention."

"Well, you've got it now. Come back to Rodey."

"When?"

"Tonight."

"Tonight?" She sighed and leaned over to rest her elbows on the counter, the egg still in her hand. If she wasn't careful, she would find herself with a handful of yolk.

"Next weekend."

She held her breath for a second. Chantele had no idea where this might lead, but she wanted to go. Even if they only picked back up where they left off, sparring about the future or the things they valued, she wanted to go.

“I’ll call you later,” he told her. “But I wanna see pictures of that breakfast.”

When he ended the call, Chantele stood for a moment, heart in her throat. And her fingertips. And her toes. Rye wanted her to come and visit him. Part of her could already imagine his arms around her, his lips on hers. But he’d already walked away from her once. Could she really put herself out there again?

“So.” Paisley cleared her throat. “Explain.”

CHAPTER SIXTEEN

CHANTELE

Chantele busied herself with the eggs for the biscuits. Her mind reeled with the call from Rye. His invitation. The fact that her two best friends were now watching her with bated breath, waiting for her to explain what was going on.

Paisley drank her juice, and Nova sipped her coffee. The only sounds in Paisley's kitchen now were the gentle taps of the glass and cup on the table each time they put them down. Even Vince, who sometimes had the TV on so loud Chantele couldn't hear herself think, was nowhere to be found.

The oven timer beeped, and Nova scooted her chair back to hurry over and get the biscuits out. The extreme silence finally made Chantele snap. She laughed as she sliced the biscuits open and arranged a fried egg on each of them.

"Where's Vince?" she asked as she set the spatula down.

"Took the car for an oil change," Paisley answered. "He'll be back."

"I'll just wrap a couple in foil to keep them warm for him."

Nova carried plates to the table for herself and Paisley as Chantele took the aluminum foil out to wrap two breakfast sandwiches.

"For Pete's sake!" Paisley nearly growled. "What is going on? Was that Rye on the phone?"

"Yes." Chantele finally poured herself a cup of coffee and carried a plate to the table to join her friends. "That was Rye on the phone."

Both of them stared at her, mouths agape, waiting for her to say more. Instead, Chantele took a big bite of her sandwich and chewed slowly. She'd never made garlic and herb biscuits, never had them. But they sounded good, so she had decided to try the recipe.

"Damn." She nodded. "That's good."

"So." Nova tipped her head. "You're talking to Rye. You're *still* talking to Rye Gallaher. The cowboy from Rodey."

Chantele nodded again.

"You know it's been almost six weeks since we were there, right?"

"Mm." Chantele smiled. "I know."

"Are you sexting?" Nova asked at the same time Paisley asked, "Why didn't you tell us?"

"Because." Chantele wiped her hands and her mouth with a napkin. "We are not sexting. We've just been talking.

Mainly, he texts me every week to ask me what I'm making you guys for breakfast."

"Seriously?" Paisley asked with a soft laugh.

"I think he's enjoying that I lost the bet a little too much," Chantele mumbled with a shrug.

"But you also talk on the phone." Nova narrowed her eyes at Chantele. "Because when you answered that call, you were like, chill, about it. Not freaked out that he called you."

"Yes, we've talked on the phone some."

Chantele sipped her coffee, wondering if maybe they hadn't heard Rye's end of the conversation. Maybe she could wiggle out of this yet. Then again, he had asked her to come and visit him. Never mind that she was supposed to fix breakfast for them next weekend. If she said she was going to Rodey, they wouldn't care. Hell, if she announced she was done with the cooking five months earlier than the bet dictated, they wouldn't blink.

But she needed to talk to them about this. Who else could she bounce this crazy idea off?

"So." Paisley shrugged. Neither of them had picked up their sandwich yet.

"Okay, we'll talk," Chantele said with a nod, "but these are delicious, and they're hot, so eat."

Nova sighed and quirked an eyebrow at her biscuit sandwich. "It does look good."

Paisley picked hers up and took a bite. She closed her eyes and moaned in appreciation.

"What did he want?" Nova asked. "When he called. What did he say?"

Still with her mouth full, Paisley nodded and pointed at Nova.

"Well, he wanted a picture."

"A dirty picture?" Nova asked quickly.

"No." Chantele rolled her eyes. Although, he had hinted around that he wouldn't mind that. "He wanted a selfie while I was cooking for you guys. I sent him one a few weeks ago when I was doing omelets at your apartment, Nova."

"You took a selfie for him at my apartment and didn't even tell us what was going on?"

"That's kind of sweet," Paisley decided. "That he wanted a selfie. A picture of you cooking."

Chantele sighed and nodded. "He is kind of...sweet. Sometimes."

"He's not normal. He didn't want a hookup. And he doesn't want dirty pictures."

Chantele swallowed a bite of her sandwich and nearly choked.

"Did you send him a picture? Of the biscuits?" Paisley asked her.

"Nope."

They ate in silence for a few minutes, Chantele wondering how to bring up his invitation. Since he'd already turned her down once, it didn't seem likely that he was asking her to come and visit so they could sleep together. And yet, most grown men she knew didn't have platonic sleepovers just for a free, homemade breakfast, either.

"So." She sipped her coffee and took a deep breath. "He just...asked me to come and see him."

This time Nova nearly choked. Paisley gave her a whack on the back and then reached for her juice. Chantele snorted, deciding Paisley was more than ready for motherhood.

"He just—? Just now?" Nova asked her.

"Yep."

"And you said what?"

"I didn't really give him an answer," she mumbled.

"Do you want to see him?" Paisley took a big bite of her sandwich and closed her eyes in appreciation.

"I think I do."

"You think?"

"Well." Chantele shrugged at Nova. "I don't know what... the invitation means. I don't know what I want. I sure don't know what he wants, because six weeks ago, he didn't want me."

"Chant—"

"Not to mention, he has a way of saying things that make me mad. Or defensive."

"What? Because he said he could picture you drinking bougie coffee?"

"Maybe."

"You do."

"I don't." Chantele lifted her mug of black coffee from the table as if to remind her friend she liked plain strong black coffee.

"But you have."

"Who hasn't?"

"The townhouse thing pissed you off, didn't it?" Paisley asked. She had slowed down on her sandwich. Chantele eyed it, noticing her friend had eaten well over half of it.

"Didn't piss me off, but I mean..." Chantele shrugged. "I don't wanna be cooped up in an apartment or even a townhouse forever."

"All things you could talk about over dinner," Nova mumbled quietly. "You know...if you went to see him."

"What if we're just not compatible?"

"What if you're not?" Nova shook her head. "Then you stay friends and move on. I mean, sounds like you're having fun texting with him. Seems like you would have fun hanging out with him."

"I thought he was miffed about the bet." Paisley scooted her chair back a bit and rested her hands on her baby bump.

"He was."

"She apologized," Nova reminded Paisley.

"I did." Chantele nodded. "It was in poor taste."

"Guys do it all the time," Nova reminded her.

"Maybe. But if the tables had been turned, and Mav had bet Rye, I'd be mad."

"True." Nova nodded her agreement. "I think you should go. And I'm okay with not having breakfast next weekend. How about you, Paisley?"

"Seriously, Chan, you don't have to do this for six months. You're making me fat."

"A bet's a bet," Chantele argued. "I'll stick to my end. But. Yeah...I might take next weekend off."

CHAPTER SEVENTEEN

RYE

Rye stared at Chantele across the cab of his truck. Singing along to a Kelsea Ballerini song, she hadn't missed a word yet. She swept her gaze from the passenger window, over the windshield, and caught him watching her.

"What?" she asked with a laugh.

"Do you like this song?"

"I do." She nodded. "Shouldn't you be watching the road?"

He couldn't believe she'd agreed to visit. Even after she called him back the day after he'd asked her, even when they finalized plans for her to drive to his place and spend the weekend, he had been surprised when she'd knocked on his door earlier this evening.

Rye had no idea what she was thinking when he led her to his spare bedroom so she could put her bags there. He wanted to sleep with her; he'd wanted to sleep with her that night she hit on him at the bar. But that whole night hadn't worked out well for either of them, and now, he wasn't sure what she would do if he came onto her.

Maybe he would find out. He planned to show her a good time and see where things went. Talking to her via text messages and phone calls was fun, but he was hoping to make the most of this visit.

He glanced at the ribbon of black in front of the truck and then peeked at her again. No longer singing, a small smile painted her face.

"Are you smiling because you're happy to be here or because you're happy to be off breakfast duty this weekend?"

Her laugh trilled through the truck like music. "Both."

"That's an insane amount of time to pay off a bet." He turned his attention back to the road. "You know that, right?"

"Mmm."

From the corner of his eye, he saw her shrug.

"Yeah. But Nova washed Paisley's car every weekend for a year, so. I don't know. Six months isn't bad. And I only do one day a weekend."

"I'm almost afraid to ask."

She was smiling at him when he looked at her again.

"Pais bet her she could out drink her one night."

"And Paisley won?"

"Nova had been traveling, so she was tired. And she was coming down with a nasty sinus infection and didn't realize it. So yeah, Nova took the bet. Paisley was drunk as a skunk, but still standing. Nova passed out at the table."

"Were you at a bar?"

"Yep."

"Ouch. I bet that wounded Nova's pride."

Chantele laughed again. "You have no idea. Pais doesn't usually drink a lot. And she and Vince have been married for three years, maybe? And of course, now she's pregnant, so she doesn't even go out with us much anymore."

"Where did they meet?"

"Not in a bar, if that's what you're getting at."

Rye chuckled and shook his head. "Nope. Just curious."

"He knew one of her cousins. Went to school with him. They met at a football game, I think. Dated for a couple of years before they got married."

The conversation stopped at a comfortable stand still, and the Kelsea Ballerini song changed to Luke Combs.

"Where are we going?"

"Dinner."

When she didn't answer him, he glanced at her, not surprised when she rolled her eyes at him.

"Where is dinner?"

Chantele Morgan was a little bit feisty. Damned if Rye didn't like that. Hell, he might have been more attracted to that the first night at the bar than her pretty eyes and sweet little curves.

"Watch the road!" She gave him a playful swat and shook her head. "You can't look at me like that."

"I am watching the road," he promised her. "And how am I looking at you?"

"Like you like what you see."

"I very much like what I see, Chantele," he said quietly.

"What changed your mind?"

"I liked everything I saw that night at the Iron Stag." He nodded. "I told you. I'm too old for the games. For the hookups."

He glanced at her again, saw that she was thinking it over, possibly trying to decide how to respond. Eventually, she nibbled on her lower lip and said nothing at all.

"Dinner is at Lockland Distilling."

"Really?" Her face lit up with her smile. "I bought their five-year bourbon that weekend. And then I was pissed that I did."

"Why?"

"Because you bought me the pour, and I was mad at you."

"Because I didn't want to be your boy toy."

"Because you didn't want me."

"There's a difference." He shook his head. "You know that."

"Might be a little late for it to matter."

Rye slowed as he neared the turn for Lockland. He looked at her, recognizing the challenge in her eyes. She was attracted to him, but she wasn't going to be easily persuaded into anything. Now this he liked.

Game on.

CHAPTER EIGHTEEN

CHANTELE

Chantele had come to Lockland on the girls' weekend, but they hadn't taken any tours or even gone to the Skeleton Bar. They'd made a quick round through the gift shop, bought the bourbon, and headed back out. As much as they liked the distilleries, they had chosen to go to Kissing Springs for the boutiques. And the male-revue.

Now, though, with Rye, she walked through the gift shop at a casual pace. Rye sauntered straight over to the wall of bottles and studied the offerings. He was dressed in denim that looked soft and comfortable, but Chantele wouldn't know. She hadn't come close to touching him since that quick hug when he opened his door to her earlier.

He wore a neat black t-shirt that stretched tight over his broad shoulders and capped those upper arms in a perfect display. She wasn't sure if she missed the cowboy hat or if she appreciated the sight of his longish, curly blond hair without it. Both were good looks. There was still something about the way he wore his jeans and the black boots that screamed cowboy. Not that it mattered anymore. The bet was over and done, and she would pay the loss without complaint.

But Chantele liked this cowboy and was enjoying the view.

Hands in his pockets, he turned and looked at her over his shoulder. She put down the candle she was looking at and moseyed over to stand beside him.

"How many of these bottles do you have?" she asked him.

"Just a couple." He pointed at the two—one being the same she'd bought and the other a single barrel.

They wandered through the gift shop together, stopping whenever one of them picked something up to look at it closer. Chantele considered buying a sweatshirt, but since it was summer, she decided against it. Maybe if she came back in the fall. If she had a reason to come back.

"Are you ready to eat?" he asked her.

"Yeah." She nodded as they crossed the shop to the main door.

"Hey."

Rye stopped walking when the male voice carried across the room.

"Knox." He turned with a grin and shook hands with the guy who approached them. "How ya doin'?"

"Good." The guy nodded. "Good to see you. What's going on?"

Rye turned to Chantele with a smile. "Just going over to get something to eat."

"At the Skeleton?" Knox grinned. Chantele liked that he seemed pleased, that he was proud of the place.

"Chantele, this is Knox Lockland. We went to school together." Rye gestured to Chantele, barely brushing her shoulder with his fingertips. "Knox, this is my friend, Chantele Morgan. She's from Lexington. Thought she would enjoy the Skeleton."

"Nice to meet you." Knox reached for her hand.

"And you." She shook his hand and then folded her arms over her chest.

"You're gonna love it. Have you been in there lately?" Knox turned and directed that question at Rye.

"No. I'm either workin' or at the Iron Stag watching Mav work the room."

Knox snorted and shook his head. "He hasn't changed a bit."

"He hasn't," Rye agreed.

"Well, my sister's back in the area. She and I are working on some updates in the bar. Little bit of redecorating. Getting some new events on the calendar. I think you'll like the changes."

Chantele flicked her gaze to Rye, curious what he would say.

"How's she doing?"

"Good." Another big smile. "She's seein' Taj Bailey."

"Wow." Rye nodded. "I heard that. How's that make you big brothers feel?"

Knox snorted softly again. "Luckily, he's good to her, so it hasn't been an issue."

The guys shared a laugh.

"Enjoy your dinner," Knox told them. "Good to see you, Rye."

"You, too."

Knox moved away as quickly as he'd appeared, already talking to the girl behind the reception counter. Rye pushed the door open and nodded for Chantele to step outside. The early evening sun was still warm. Chantele breathed deeply through her nose, inhaling the scent of the coming summer, outdoors, and the corn and mash that always hung in the air in this part of Kentucky.

"Let me guess." She peeked at him as they started walking across the sidewalk to a building made of the same dark cedar as the gift shop. The sign above the door said Skeleton Bar. She was curious about the name, but she would wait until they were seated before asking. "Once upon a time you had a crush on Knox's sister."

"Everyone had a crush on Summer Lockland at some point in school." He shrugged easily. "And no one dared to get near her because of her brothers."

"How many?"

"Three. Knox is my age. Branch is a few years older. And Cole is a few years younger. Nice guys, but they know how to handle themselves in a fight."

Chantele rolled her eyes. “Why do guys fight?”

“Why do girls do the silent treatment and bicker and take cheap shots at each other?”

“Good point.” She nodded.

When Rye opened the door for her again, she led him inside. They stopped at the hostess stand, but Chantele eyed the bar with interest. She liked the vibe. A young woman with long, wavy dark hair stood with a shaker in her hands, talking to an older couple at the end of the bar. She offered them a dazzling smile and then shook whatever drink she was making.

“Follow me.”

Chantele looked back at the hostess as she led them deep into the bar to a two-top table near a wall of windows.

“Would you like to sit outside?” she offered. “I can put you out there on the deck, or I can seat you right here.”

Rye glanced at Chantele. “Up to you.”

“Outside is good.”

“Right this way.” The girl led them out to a two-top on the deck and placed their menus on the table. “Someone will be right with you.”

“Thanks.” Rye nodded. Before Chantele could move, he stepped around her and pulled her chair out for her. She studied his face as she sat down, wondering if he was naturally polite and chivalrous or if he was trying to win points with her. Then again, why would he bother?

"What's good here?" She picked up the menu but looked at him.

"Everything, really. Depends on what you like."

"Is the chicken sandwich good?"

"Definitely one of my favorites."

"Hmm." She nodded.

"The woodfire pizza is really good, too."

"Oh. That sounds good."

"Want to share one?"

"I do." She opened the menu and scanned it until she saw the pizza choices. "What do you like on yours?"

He shot her a slow grin. "We're gonna clash here, aren't we?"

"We're bound to," she answered simply.

"Meat."

Chantele rolled her eyes. "I can deal with that. What about green peppers?"

"I can pick them off." He shrugged as if to say no big deal.

"Well, look at that. We agreed right off the bat."

"We compromised," he corrected her.

"What about pineapple?"

"You're one of those people?" His severe frown made her chuckle.

"What people?"

"People who think pineapple goes on anything other than a plate?"

"I like it on pizza. In salads sometimes. Dips. Smoothies."

"Yeah, no." Rye shook his head. "Here's the clash."

"I can do without it on the pizza," she promised.

"Hey."

They looked up when a pretty blonde approached the table with a big smile.

"I'm Summer. I'm going to take care of you tonight." She tipped her head and studied Rye's face for a moment. "You look familiar."

"Went to school with Knox."

"Mm." Summer snorted. "You have my sympathy."

"Rye Gallaher."

"Oh yeah!" She nodded with enthusiasm. "I remember you. You played basketball with Knox, didn't you? And you dated Kaley Ludwig?"

Rye laughed and nodded. "Yes, I did. Both."

"What's she doing now?"

"No idea. I think she went to school in Tennessee, but I haven't seen or heard from her since."

Summer nodded. "Funny. Time flies. I'm sorry. I'm talking, and you guys probably want to order."

"It's fine." Rye nodded his head over the table at Chantele. "This is my friend, Chantele Morgan. Chantele, Summer Lockland."

"Nice to meet you." Summer favored her with a friendly smile. "Did you go to school here?"

"No. I'm from Indiana. I live in Lexington now."

"Our bartender's from Indiana!" Summer grinned and then laughed at herself. "I know. That doesn't mean you know her. What can I get you to drink?"

"Can I get a Kentucky Mule?"

"Absolutely. Rye?"

"I'll do the same."

"Okay. I'll get your drink orders in while you look over the menu."

"Thank you."

CHAPTER NINETEEN

Rye

"So, you were in band?" Rye tipped his head and narrowed his eyes at her. "Really?"

"Yes, really. Why is that so hard to believe?"

"You just don't look like a piccolo player."

"Flute," she corrected him.

"Aren't they the same?"

"Similar, but no."

"Can you play the piccolo?"

"Yeah." Chantele took a drink. The Kentucky Mules had been a good idea; Rye had considered just ordering a beer. But the cold drink was refreshing. He also figured if he had ordered a beer, Chantele would have ribbed him to no end since they were at a bourbon bar. "Well. I haven't played either in years, so I probably would not play either well."

"When I was in high school, band people—"

"Weren't cool." She finished for him, eyebrows arched. "Is that what you were going to say?"

He shrugged. "Maybe."

"So, you were an athlete. When I was in high school, they were jerks."

Rye laughed.

"Tell me about Kaley Ludwig."

"We dated for two years," he answered, deadpan.

"Was she your first?"

"Girlfriend?"

"Don't play dumb." Chantele shook her head.

"She was."

"Pretty?"

"Why does that matter?" He drew back with a frown, almost as if she had slapped him.

"You wanted to know what Johnny looked like."

Rye leaned forward and took another piece of their pizza. They'd just about killed it, only three pieces remained on the sheet.

"Kaley was cute," he answered. "She had short black hair. Like...I dunno what the cut was called. Just short around her face. Big green eyes."

"Was she a cheerleader?"

“Yes.”

“I thought you were a cowboy, not a jock that dated a cheerleader.”

“Disappointed?”

Chantele laughed softly.

“Why the Skeleton Bar?”

“What?” He looked around. There were five more tables on the deck, three of them were occupied. Conversation buzzed around them, and piped-in country music played quietly in the background. “You don’t like it?”

“I love it.” She hurried to reassure him. “Why the name?”

“Oh.” Rye took a bite and chewed for a moment. “Like a skeleton key. Lockland Distilling. Lock and key.”

“Okay.” Chantele nodded. “That makes sense.”

“What do you want to do tomorrow?”

She looked around and shrugged. “You’re the tour guide, Rye.”

“Are you making breakfast?”

Her laugh bubbled up from deep inside and exploded out of her smile.

“I can if you want me to.”

“I’m kidding.”

“I make a mean bowl of cereal.”

“What would happen if you didn’t want to do the next several months of cooking?”

"Nothing." She shrugged. "But I won't quit. I have to save face. You turned me down."

Rye sighed. "You know it wasn't that simple."

"Pretty simple."

"You didn't find another cowboy? You went to the strip club thing in Kissing Springs, right?"

"We did." She smiled. "Fun. But no. Do you really think I wanted to take a stripper home?"

"You wanted to take a cowboy home."

"Never gonna let me live that down, are you?"

"Imagine us telling our grandchildren about how we met."

"Grandchildren?" she repeated. "Are you crazy?"

"Guess we'll see," he answered. "Do you want another drink?"

"I'm good."

Rye quirked an eyebrow at her. "Do you want to go to the Iron Stag and ride Bogart?" He wasn't sure why he was baiting her like this. Maybe he hoped she would flirt back and ask if her riding Bogart would interest him this time. When she only gave him a frosty look, he laughed softly.

"How about you give me the tour?"

"Of Rodey?" he asked with wide eyes. "You've seen it."

The amusement on her face was priceless.

"Show me where you went to school."

"Okay." He shrugged.

They stood at the same time, and Rye ushered her to walk ahead of him. He'd paid their bill a while ago, but neither of them had been ready to leave at that time. He'd tipped Summer well; he would have like to have told her goodbye, but as he and Chantele left through the bar, Summer was nowhere in sight. The place was busy, though, and it was nearing closing time. Happy he had run into Knox and Summer, too, Rye pushed the door open for Chantele, and they walked side-by-side out to the parking lot.

The tour of Rodey was mostly over by the time he'd left his driveway, but he was game to hop in his truck and ride around with her for a while. At her door, he pulled it open for her and then waited for her to climb in. When he hoisted himself up into the driver's seat, he started the truck and fiddled with the radio.

"Eric Church!" She nodded when the familiar voice filled the cab of the truck.

"You like him?"

"Don't you?"

"I do," he answered. "Would you sleep with him?"

"Seriously?"

Rye chuckled at the scrunch of her nose and the frown on her face as he put the truck in gear and pulled out of the space.

"Is that a no?"

"Are you gonna ask me that about everyone now?"

"No." He slung his left wrist over the top of the steering wheel and drove the truck out of the lot to the highway. "What's going on with Nova and Maverick?"

"Beats me."

"It's weird. Mav doesn't do the whole long-distance thing."

"I don't think they're a thing."

"Still. He doesn't do long distance relationships. Hell, he doesn't do *relationships*. It's totally not like him to stay in touch with someone he hasn't slept with."

When his words were met with silence, Rye peeked at her and found her frowning, looking like she was deep in thought. "What?"

"That was almost like a math problem," she said with a shudder.

"See that barn over there?" He pointed across the cab to a dilapidated barn out her window.

"The one that looks like it would fall over if you sneezed on it?"

"That's the one," he answered with a nod.

"What about it?"

"We used to throw parties there."

"Who owns it?"

"No idea. But we had some good times there. Police finally busted us after several years."

"How old were you?" She snorted.

“Started partying there when I was probably sixteen. Police showed up when I was about nineteen, maybe?”

“Did you go to college?”

“Is that a box you’re checking off?”

Chantele sighed and rested her head on the seat.

“No. I’m just asking.”

“Community college. I was kind of interested in engineering, but my parents didn’t have the money to send me to a big school. And I was already working for Robert by then.”

“Robert.”

“Mav’s dad. He owns one of the biggest ranches in the area.”

“So, you’re an honest-to-God, no kidding cowboy?”

“I am.” He nodded.

“But you don’t live in a bunkhouse? On the property?”

“Nope. Robert’s bunkhouse is small. There’re a couple guys that live there. But most of us are close enough, we have our own places.”

“Do you travel much?”

“No. I don’t.”

“If you could go anywhere tomorrow, where would you go?”

Rye stopped himself before he could say something dumb. That he would go anywhere with her. Odds were, she would slap him. But she interested him in ways the women in his life up until now didn't.

"I'd like to see the coast, I guess. Never been to the ocean."

From the corner of his eye, he saw her nod.

"What about you?" he asked.

"I'd like to see the Northeast in the fall."

"The leaves?"

"Yeah. I love fall. I think that would be pretty."

Eyes on her, Rye only nodded. He understood the draw. He liked to look at pretty things, too.

CHAPTER TWENTY

CHANTELE

Chantele was surprised to wake to the smell of coffee brewing in the morning. Then again, everything about Rye Gallaher had been a surprise. When he'd showed her to the spare bedroom yesterday when she first arrived, she wondered if he was kidding. But when they'd come back to his place last night after driving around and talking for an hour after eating, he'd said goodnight and they'd gone to separate rooms.

She showered and dressed before joining Rye in the kitchen, only to find her next surprise. Dressed in the uniform of denim and the snug-fitting t-shirt with an apron tied around his waist, Rye had greeted her with a smile, a good morning, and the offer to fix her breakfast.

She sipped coffee while Rye made eggs and sausage. Chantele asked if he had been up long, if he'd gone to the ranch to work earlier, but Rye told her Robert had given him the weekend for her visit. When he suggested they go to the ranch for a ride, she asked if he meant a four-wheeler. When he corrected her and said he meant horseback riding, she had nearly choked on her coffee.

And yet, after breakfast—and Chantele supposed eggs and sausage weren't gourmet, but Rye did both well—they had packed up his truck and gone to the ranch. Rye had led her around the grounds, sharing tidbits of information about the lands and boundaries and memories about all the times he and Mav had shared out there through the years.

He'd walked her through the horse barn. Introduced her to so many horses, Chantele had forgotten their names before they were done. He introduced her to a few of the ranch hands, too. Chantele had worried about what she would say if they bumped into Maverick. It seemed obvious that she was here to sleep with Rye, at least she'd assumed that was the point of the weekend. And as much as that embarrassed her—if the guys here all knew that she was spending the weekend at Rye's—the fact that she was spending the weekend in the spare bedroom at Rye's was worse.

He'd selected Rosebud for her and promised Chantele she was a gentle mare. Rye had talked to Rosebud in a soft, almost seductive voice as he smoothed his hand down her nose. Then he'd invited Chantele to do the same. Rosebud had thrilled her when she leaned into her touch.

"What do you think?" he asked quietly. "You ready to try this?"

"Sure," she mumbled. Nerves tickled her belly, but she was excited. She wanted to try this. Imagine going home and telling Nova and Paisley she had gone horseback riding.

"What do you think we need to do first?"

"Drink." She shot him a big grin.

Rye laughed and shook his head. "We gotta saddle Rosebud."

"You don't ride bareback?"

He hesitated as he stepped away from her, presumably to get a saddle.

"I can," he said with a nod. "And I do, sometimes. But we'll go with saddles."

She smirked as he walked away. Kind of dumb to try innuendo with him, since he'd already turned her down. But she couldn't help it. Something about Rye Gallaher made it fun to push the limits, to get under his skin. Skin she would still very much like to touch, but obviously, he wasn't interested in getting to know her that way.

He returned with a brush and what looked like a rug or a pad.

"Okay." He grinned at her as he stopped beside her. "First thing we're gonna do is brush Rosebud. If she sweats, and she has loose hair, she'll shake to get rid of the hair and throw you off."

"Good to know." Chantele nodded.

Rye stroked the brush over her shoulder and flank, murmuring to her as he worked. Chantele loved the soft sound of his voice, the way the horse turned her head his way, as if to listen to him sweet talk her. Chantele understood that; she figured she would do the same if Rye spoke to her that way.

"You wanna do this side?"

"Yes." Chantele stepped up beside him and took the brush when he handed it to her. Much to her surprise, he stepped up behind her and covered her hand with his. Together they moved the brush over the mare's shoulder and flank. Rosebud stood calmly as they worked.

"Next, we need to check the saddle pad. Make sure there's nothing sharp stuck to it that would hurt her."

Chantele watched him work. This was nice. Watching him work, watching him interact with a horse. Out here in the open, his boots and jeans and hat were more than costume pieces, more than glitter to draw a woman's interest. Chantele watched the muscles in his back flex as he moved, listening as he continued to talk to her about each step. Funny that she'd been attracted to him at the bar. Seeing him in his real world made her that much more attracted to him, but it also rubbed a little salt in the wound of embarrassment.

She'd picked him out at the bar because of the stereotype of rugged, handsome cowboys. He was that, for sure, but she sensed from the way he walked the land and handled the horses, he was so much more. Chantele made herself look away for a moment when he had Rosebud saddled and ready for her. The gentle touch of his hand on the horse's shoulder did something funny to Chantele's insides.

Wasn't going to do her any good to catch feelings here. Maybe they were friends. Maybe this trip was meant to set her and her friends straight about the way women looked at men—what a turnaround from the usual narrative—and maybe he had just wanted to school Chantele on horses. But Rye Gallaher had no interest in anything more with her.

Once Rosebud was saddled and ready, Rye went through the same steps with a sleek black horse he called Fleet. Nervous but ready, Chantele listened as Rye instructed her on how to mount the horse. He held Rosebud steady as Chantele took the reins in her left hand and put her left foot up in the stirrup.

“Good.” Rye nodded. He spoke in that same calm tone to her that he'd used with Rosebud. “Now. You're gonna pull up like you're standing. Right leg's gonna hang there by your left leg. Then you'll just swing it over. Careful not to kick her. When you sit, be gentle.”

“Okay.”

Chantele did as he told her, thrilled as she moved through the steps and finally, gently, sat in the saddle.

“Put your right foot in the stirrup,” he instructed her. He nodded as she did so and then checked the lengths of the stirrups. “Okay. You ready to do this? We'll go slow. We'll just do a nice walk through that pasture. It's nice and even.”

Chantele glanced at the unending field out behind the barn and nodded.

“Next time you come, I'm gonna quiz you on saddling.”

“Just don't quiz me on the other horses' names.”

“Does that mean you're gonna have issues at my family reunions?”

“Are you telling me your family is horses?”

“Sometimes some of them are horses' asses.” He grinned up at her. “We need to get you a hat, too. Maybe some boots.”

"Really?" She leaned a tiny bit to look at her running shoe in the stirrup.

"Mm-hmm. We'll do a little more than a walk next time, too."

Next time. He kept referencing next time. She hoped there would be a next time, but she was still confused. She wanted more than friendship with him, even after he'd turned her down flat and walked away from her at the Iron Stag. No way she would throw herself at him again, though. So, if she did come back, Chantele would have to figure out how to deal with her growing feelings for him.

She watched with interest as Rye took Fleet's reins and hauled himself up in the saddle with ease. Damned if he didn't look that much more delicious on horseback.

"Keep your reins loose," Rye told her. "And sit back in the saddle. Don't kick her. But give her a gentle squeeze with your legs to let her know you want her to walk."

Chantele held her breath, but Fleet stepped even closer to her, and Rye reached for her hand.

"Relax."

His voice was gentle, but that touch of his hand on hers didn't do a damned thing to relax her. She nodded and when Rye let go of her hand and Fleet moved away, she gave Rosebud a gentle squeeze.

"Wow." She threw Rye a quick grin when the horse started walking.

CHAPTER TWENTY-ONE

Rye

Rye loved the look of accomplishment on Chantele's face as they walked the horses through the pasture behind the barn. The genuine smile was as beautiful as he had assumed it would be, but it was more. The sun, the thrill of the moment, put a little color in her cheeks, and her eyes sparkled with excitement.

They rode for a while, swapping stories about their jobs, families, and friends. The more Chantele talked, the more it surprised him that she'd made a play for him at the Iron Stag all those weeks ago. She didn't seem the type to go on the prowl for a one-night stand. She was close to her family, and she loved her friends.

He supposed that was what had done it. Sent her to the bar that night to make eyes at him. Whether she had found him attractive or not, she had that bet with friends, and it sounded like the three of them took their bets seriously.

She asked a few questions about Maverick, but Rye honestly didn't get the sense that she was interested in him. Actually, it sounded like she didn't want to bump into him, because she was embarrassed about what had happened at the Iron Stag.

After dismounting, Chantele took her phone out to take some pictures of the barn and the horses while Rye took care of the cool-down process. He felt her watching him as he worked. She loved the horses. He'd been a cowboy long enough to read people around horses. She had been nervous, but she'd done well, and now, she was admiring the grace and the beauty of the horses as well as the rolling bluegrass and the crisp blue skies.

Rye just hoped she was still interested in looking at him. She'd asked him about riding bareback earlier. He thought she was teasing him, throwing a little sexual innuendo at him, but he wasn't sure.

"Are you hungry?" he asked her when he had attended to both horses.

"A little bit," she admitted.

"Wanna ride into Kissing Springs? Grab some lunch?"

"Yeah, sounds good."

On the drive, he felt her sidelong looks. Caught her watching him once. Country music filled the cab of the truck, but Rye was more interested in the small sounds she made. She yawned a few times. Coughed once. Sang along with most of the songs playing. But Rye could have sworn he heard her breathing, that his own body, his lungs, were in tune with her.

He took her to Hope's Diner in Kissing Springs. Nothing fancy, but damned good food. They had shakes and burgers, and when they finished eating, and Chantele said she was stuffed, Rye still insisted they go to Minnie's Pie Shop.

"I can't eat another bite," Chantele protested.

"We can share," he offered. They walked the square in the booming little town. Rye had been in and out of Kissing Springs many times, enough that some people looked familiar. But he didn't know anyone well. Living in Rodey, there wasn't much around his place for entertainment. If he wasn't up for driving to Louisville or Lexington, he could usually find something to do in Kissing Springs.

"I don't need pie on my hips."

He eyed her with a grin as they walked. "I was thinking more that we could just eat it."

She laughed and slapped at him.

"Wanna stay here tonight? See the male-revue again?"

"I don't. No." She shook her head.

"Was it a good show, though?"

"You thinkin' about going?'

"Just asking."

"Yeah." She shrugged. "It was fun."

"Been to other male-revues?"

"Once. In Vegas."

"How'd it compare?"

"Actually, I liked the one here better," she decided.

"Interesting."

"You ever think about joining the show? Auditioning? Whatever?"

"Me?" He snorted and rolled his eyes. "Not a chance in hell."

"What kind of pie is good here?" she asked as they neared Minnie's.

"All of it," he answered.

"Because I'm not sharing pecan pie with you."

"Pee-can," he corrected her.

"Whatever."

"What do you wanna do for dinner tonight?" he asked her.

"Seriously? I don't think I need to eat until tomorrow afternoon."

"Can I cook for you?"

He had the evening planned, but he wasn't going to tell her that. Rye had purchased steaks to grill, ingredients for a pasta salad, and a bottle of wine. He wasn't much into wine, but he wanted to be prepared in case she was. If not, he had a brand-new bottle of Lockland Five Year ready to open and share.

And that was only the beginning of his plans.

He'd dated. He'd been with a few women, though never as many as Maverick. But Rye had never seduced a woman. Tonight, he planned to go the distance. He hoped Chantele was still attracted to him, maybe seeing him cowboy out on Robert's ranch had turned her on. Rye would use his charm and his wit and hopefully some kissing—they'd already shared those kisses weeks ago, and he was still thinking about them—to get Chantele to put her guard down. If it were up to him, she wouldn't be sleeping in the guest room tonight.

CHAPTER TWENTY-TWO

Chantele

Sharing a slice of apple pie with Rye put Chantele over the edge, so she was happy to walk around Kissing Springs a while longer. Anything to work the extra calories off. Chantele wasn't even terribly worried about the calories; she was simply miserably stuffed.

Minnie's Pie Shop did a good business, and even as Chantele's stomach protested as she ate her part of the slice of apple, she had to admit the flaky, buttery crust and the sweet apple filling was delicious. She reminded herself not to be childish when Rye had offered her the first bite—from the same fork he would be using. But she had still watched him, butterflies raging in her belly, when he slipped that fork in his mouth and then licked his lips. And she'd still flipped out a bit when she took her next bite. True, they'd shared a couple of steamy kisses—well, she thought they were steamy, anyway—but those had happened weeks ago. Over a month ago.

And it hadn't escaped Chantele's notice that even though Rye had invited her here for the weekend, he hadn't kissed her this time.

After the pie was gone, they walked the square again and then wandered down to the Love Lock Bridge. Chantele had seen bridges like this, intricate metalworks woven together, with padlocks attached everywhere, but she'd never heard any stories or history about them. Rye didn't seem to know much more than she did, but he did tell her something about a lady mayor and a pillar of the community falling in love years ago and the guy having the bridge built for her.

Apparently, when a couple was in love, they hooked a lock on the bridge and threw away the key. Rye hadn't really joked when he told her the story, but she could feel the doubt rolling off him in waves. She wondered if he didn't believe in true love or if he just thought the tradition was silly.

Chantele thought it was sweet.

She fought sleep on the drive back to Rodey. Rye even told her to relax and take a nap, but naturally, that made her sit up and pretend to be bright-eyed. When they arrived at his house and Rye killed the truck engine, Chantele took a moment to look around. It was still light out the night before when she'd come here, but she hadn't taken much time to admire his place.

The bricked ranch-style home was small, though she would say charming. She supposed it was an older house, but Rye kept it neat. She'd already seen how tidy the inside of the house was, not even a speck of dust in the spare bedroom. Though, she suspected he had probably cleaned for her arrival. Eyes on the landscaping in front of the house, she climbed out of the truck.

Little green plants that she thought were stove pipe yews lined the front under the picture window. Colored rock surrounded the plants. Two planters with beautiful-colored flowers climbing and falling over the edges decorated the small front stoop. Chantele couldn't keep flowers like that alive, even if she did have a front porch to display them.

"Do you do your own yard work?" She leaned on the closed truck door and glanced at him as he rounded the grill of the truck to stand by her.

"You think I'd hire it out?"

She shrugged, a small grin playing at her lips.

"I wasn't sure you'd have the time to deal with it," she said sincerely. "And also, I'm a little bit jealous. I do not have a green thumb."

"I make time for things I like."

His words chased a shiver up her spine, but damned if she wanted him to see it.

"How much land do you have here?"

"Coupla acres," he answered. "I'm on the backside of my parents' property."

"Really?" She looked around, curious now where his parents lived.

"Yeah. That way. Lots of wooded acres between us."

"Nice."

"C'mon." He reached for her hand and led her around the side of the house. She flexed her fingers in his despite telling herself not to make a big deal of the touch. He didn't mean anything by it; he wanted her to follow him. But even when they stood in the backyard and Chantele was admiring his patio—a two-top table with an umbrella, a gathering of two cushioned chairs and a loveseat around a firepit, and more potted flowers—he still held her hand.

"I like it."

"What's your place like?" he asked.

"I rent," she answered. "I'm on the second floor of a duplex house."

"But not a townhouse."

She snorted softly.

"Who's got your dog this weekend?"

"Paisley and Vince."

"You could bring him with you next time."

Chantele looked up as Rye stepped closer to her. Fingers of one hand still linked with hers, he lifted his other hand and brushed his fingers over her cheek. Those same butterflies that had stirred over sharing a fork, like they were in fifth grade instead of responsible adults, fluttered again. Would he kiss her now?

"Will there be a next time?" she asked him.

"I hope so." He nodded. "After all, we barely got into a trot with Rosebud and Fleet today."

She tipped her head trying to hide the goofy smile. Right now, she wanted to talk about the two of them. About what might be going on between them. Right now, she wanted him to kiss her. But she had loved the horses. Her nerves had melted away shortly after mounting Rosebud. The mare was gentle, and Rye was clearly in charge.

"So." He gave her fingers a squeeze and let go of her hand. "What's the next bet? The next big dare?"

"For me?" The shift in conversation and the absence of his touch left her reeling.

"They'll get you again? Don't you guys like take turns?"

"Um." She frowned and followed him when he started back around the house. "We don't take turns, but...It's more of a spur of the moment kind of thing."

"What kind of spur of the moment kind of thing ended up with your dare to ride a cowboy?"

He unlocked the door and motioned her inside.

"Do you like wine?"

"It's okay, I guess," she answered with a shrug.

"Would you rather have a glass of wine or a pour of Lockland?"

Chantele stared at him blankly when they reached the kitchen, and he took the two bottles from a cabinet and set them on the counter.

"Which would you—"

"You choose."

She took a deep breath and studied each of the bottles. “Let’s do wine.”

“Wine it is,” he agreed. She watched him open the bottle with ease, surprised when he pulled two wine glasses from a different cabinet. “What?”

“What do you mean?”

“I saw the look on your face,” he said with a grin. He poured the red in each glass and then set the bottle aside. “You’re surprised I have wine glasses.”

“Kind of,” she whispered, although the laugh that followed was louder.

“I borrowed them from my mother,” he confessed. “Can’t impress a city girl pouring good red wine into plastic cups.”

Chantele took the cup he offered her and met his eyes.

“You’re trying to impress me?”

“Maybe.”

Rather than comment further, Chantele sipped the wine and nodded her approval.

“Is it working?”

Eyes locked with his, she smiled.

“Maybe.”

“Do you like living in the city?”

She took a deep breath, thrown again by the change of topic.

“Yes and no.” She leaned on the counter and folded her arms over her chest. “I mean, I like it. I like my life. My job. My friends. Even my place.”

“But?”

“It’s not where I see myself ending up.”

“The long haul.”

She laughed softly. “Careful there.”

“What exactly about what I said that night made you mad? I mean, I think townhouses are pretty neat lookin’.”

She shrugged. “They are. I think it was more the me getting married and me and my husband reading the newspaper together. Drinking bougie coffee.”

“It was the coffee comment,” he mumbled.

“I’m not—I’m not that person. That you painted that night.”

“I didn’t know you then.”

“Exactly.”

“And yet, you wanted me to drop my pants and fuck you against the back wall of the bar.”

Chantele blew out a sharp breath and put her glass on the counter.

“I apologized, Rye. Yes, if the roles would have been reversed, and I had seen your post referencing a lost bet, I would have been offended.” She shrugged. “What more can I say?”

"Maybe I need to confess that if I hadn't seen that damned text message, I might have wanted to do exactly that."

Chantele quirked an eyebrow at him.

"You said you're not into hookups. That you're looking for more."

"I am looking for more," he confirmed. "I did all that crazy shit when I was younger. I watch all the young guys at the ranch doing all the crazy shit now. Hell, even Mav's still living that life. I don't wanna do that anymore."

"I get it," she said quietly.

"But that doesn't mean I'm not interested in you."

"I'm sleeping in the guest bedroom," she reminded him. "And the closest we've come to a kiss this weekend is sharing the same—"

Rye struck with the speed of a viper but the finesse of a man who had loved and admired his fair share of women. His lips were hot on hers, the firm pressure stealing her breath away. She gasped softly, and Rye took it as an invitation. His tongue flicked over her lips and into her mouth, stroking, searching.

She kissed him back, hands reaching for his arms to steady herself. Fingers hovering over him, she finally touched him and slid her hands up over his shoulders to link them behind his neck.

"What?" she whispered when he pulled away.

"This is all wrong."

“What?” She drew back to look at him, afraid he had already changed his mind. If he walked away again, Chantele would pack her bags. And there wouldn’t be a next time. “What do you mean? You don’t want—”

“Oh, I want.” The look in his eyes was a textbook smolder if she’d ever seen one. “But I wanted to romance you tonight. Wine you. Dine you. Sweep you off your feet with compliments and kisses and then get to this part.”

“Well, I mean, you wined me. Right? There’s wine.” She quirked an eyebrow and gave him a hopeful grin.

Rye pressed close again, stealing a quick kiss this time.

“Do you have any idea how many times I’ve relived those kisses? How hard it’s been to keep my hands to myself since you got here?”

“I don’t want you to keep your hands to yourself.” She pressed into him, thrilling at his erection against her middle. “Can we just do this part, and then we can go back and do that other stuff? The dining and the compliments and more kissing?”

CHAPTER TWENTY-THREE

Rye

To hell with the sexy, slow seduction Rye had planned. Maybe next time. With the taste of Chantele's kiss still on his mouth, her body pressed to his, and her fingers brushing the back of his neck, all thought was gone. Sliding his hands around her waist, her tugged her in harder, closer, and kissed her again.

She tasted like red wine and apple pie, and Rye wasn't sure he would ever find something so delectable again. Her hair brushed his face when he kissed a trail from her mouth down her neck, her warm skin pressed to his.

Greedy for more of her, he spread his hands over her denim clad butt and cupped her cheeks. His possessive squeeze earned him a soft moan; Rye felt her warm breath over his face.

"Better this way," he decided as he molded his hands lower around her butt and kneaded her cheeks and her thighs.

"What?"

"If we'd done this six weeks ago, I couldn't do this."

"Do what?"

Rather than answer her, Rye scooped her up in his arms.

"Good girl." He kissed a spot under her ear when she wound her legs around his waist and locked her ankles at his back. With his bedroom the destination in mind, he carried her as far as the hall. Her hands roamed his back, one over his shoulder and the other up under his arm. She smoothed her palms over him and then pawed at him, as if desperate to feel his skin.

Happy to oblige, Rye settled her against the wall, took his collar in his hands, and tugged the shirt off with one pull. He tossed it aside and worked her shirt up over her belly, an inch at a time. She shivered, jumping when he stroked his knuckles over her exposed skin.

He wanted to look, to worship, and yet with each second that passed, the need to consume every inch of her, the need to drive himself deep inside her walls and claim her as his grew wilder and more desperate. She lifted her arms allowing him to pull her shirt over her head, too.

Chantele acted with the same aggression and desperation. Her head and back pressed to the wall, she reached for the button of his jeans. Deciding there would be time for finesse and tenderness later, Rye grabbed for his wallet and plucked a condom from it, eyes still on her.

She loosened her legs around his waist and then slid her feet down to stand just long enough to unbutton her own jeans and shove them down out of his way. He caught a glimpse of black lace and then it was gone, too, discarded on her jeans on the floor.

Rye tipped his chin down for a moment to shove his jeans down over his hips and free his cock. Chantele wiggled against the wall for a second and then more black lace flashed in front of his eyes and fell to the floor. When he looked up, she was nude, her breasts high and proud, her nipples tight little pink beads.

Distracted, greedy now for the taste of her, the feel of her puckered skin on his tongue, he leaned forward and nudged the curve of her breast with his nose. Dragging his tongue over her warm, soft skin, he captured a nipple and suckled her into his mouth. Rewarded with a low moan of pleasure, he turned his attention to her other breast. Chantele took the condom from his hands. Rye moved one hand to her butt again as she lifted her legs around his waist, but with the other, he moved his briefs out of the way, and within seconds, he felt her hands stroke him and roll the condom over his cock.

Hands free of him, she lifted them and ran her fingers through his hair, pushing him closer to her breasts as he continued to play.

"Rye." She arched her back away from the wall and pulled him closer with her legs. Rye felt her heat and moved with ease, sinking into her tight, wet walls. She closed her legs tighter around him, pulling him in. Her fingers released his hair and scraped down over his back to cup his butt cheeks. Drawing him in, pushing. Clutching. He moved fast, but not so fast he couldn't drive into her hard and deep with each thrust. Chantele rode him hard, her shoulders banging hard on the wall behind her.

When he felt his balls tighten, felt lightning in his veins, he dipped his head again and took her nipple in his lips.

"I'm close," she whispered, feeling the shift in his movements, in his speed. "So close."

He closed his teeth on her nipple and bit down hard enough to make her yelp. She dropped her head against his as her body stiffened. She chanted his name, clawed her fingers back up over his shoulders and into his hair. Rye exploded inside her, yelling her name and invoking God and fate and maybe even the devil.

"Giddy up," she chuckled. "Can we do that again?"

"I've lived in Rodey all my life, and I've worn boots and a hat most of that life, and that's the first damned time any woman's ever followed up sex with a giddy up comment."

"You ever have sex on a horse?"

"No." He met her eyes, a slow grin spreading over his face. "And we're not gonna do that, either. We'd hurt the horse, and I'm pretty damned sure we'd fall off and hurt each other."

Head tipped back to rest on the wall again, Chantele closed her eyes.

"People do it in romance novels," she said with a smirk.

"You're jealous of fictional women who get fucked on the back of horses by fictional cowboys?"

She laughed softly. "No. I'm not sure I have a jealous bone in my body right now. Actually." She blinked and looked at him. "I'm not sure I have any bones in my body. I think you just melted them."

"Guess I'll have to carry you to the bedroom for round two."

"Guess so."

They remained pressed against the wall, both still too pleasure-stricken to move.

"We could have done that at the Iron Stag," she said with a thoughtful frown. "The brick would have scraped the hell out of my back, but we could have done it."

"My intention was to get you to my bed first."

"Really?" She grinned and quirked an eyebrow at him. "And you couldn't wait?"

"I couldn't wait another second." He cupped her butt cheeks in his hands and stepped back. "Know what I'm gonna do now?"

"No, but I know I'm gonna love it."

"I'm gonna put you down on my bed, and you're gonna spread those sexy thighs and show me your pussy."

"I didn't know cowboys talked like that." She leaned in and pressed her open lips to his neck.

"And then I'm gonna make you come again."

He carried her down the short hall noticing the picture frames hanging there were crooked. That made him smile. He wondered if she noticed. He turned left at the end of the hall into his bedroom and set her on the foot of the bed.

Chantele scooted back immediately and flopped backwards to lie down. Arms over her head, she parted her thighs, arched her brows, and licked her lips.

"You're right," she said softly as he knelt on the floor, slipped his hands under her thighs, and pulled her closer to the edge of the bed. The woman before him was straight from the fantasies he'd had every night since they met at the Stag six weeks ago. Too greedy to wait, Rye dipped his head and stroked his tongue up her seam.

"What am I right about?"

Chantele's eyes fluttered closed as she lifted her hips off the bed.

"It's better this way."

EPILOGUE

CHANTELE

October 2022

"You look tired."

Chantele narrowed her eyes at him while considering dropping her bag on his toes. A quick peek told her it would do no good; he was wearing his boots.

"I am tired." She chose to throw a fake punch at him instead as she stepped inside.

"Hey, hey." Rye caught her hands in his and leaned down to drop a peck on her lips. "Did you bring your hat?"

"Yes." She crossed the living room and dropped her bag on the floor in front of the couch.

"Boots?"

"I did." She nodded with a glance at her running shoes. With all the riding they did now when she visited Rye in Rodey, she was comfortable in her boots.

But still, for driving, she would choose running shoes any day.

"How's the baby?"

Chantele plopped on Rye's couch and fell back to rest.

"Absolutely precious," she answered. She closed her eyes, but when she felt Rye sit next to her on the couch, she opened them again to look at him.

"Paisley?"

"She's good." Chantele nodded. "Exhausted. You think I look bad."

"Nope." Rye cupped her face and leaned in to kiss her. "I didn't say that. I said you look tired."

She was exhausted. And yes, she had baby fever now that Tucker had arrived. She and Nova spent as much time as they could with Paisley, when Vince was at work, to help her out. They cleaned and did laundry, they cooked, and their favorite duty was holding and feeding Tucker so Paisley could rest. Chantele didn't even mind changing diapers, but that might be because she loved to count Tucker's baby toes each time she slipped a onesie off him.

"Nova still over there with you all the time?"

"Mmm." She nodded. "Yeah. She said to tell you she's scarred from you sexting me last weekend."

"Maybe she shouldn't be picking up your phone."

Chantele laughed softly. "I fell asleep in the rocker with Tucker. I don't think Nova even considered what she might see when she glanced at my phone."

"What about the first weekend in December? Did you invite them?"

"I did." Chantele kicked her shoes off and curled her legs under her on the couch. She twisted a bit to see Rye better. "I think they want to come for dinner. Paisley's mom is going to watch Tucker. Nova might stay for the weekend, but I doubt Pais and Vince do."

"I'll make reservations."

"Where are we taking them to dinner?"

"I thought we could do Two Fourteen in Kissing Springs for dinner. And we could take them to Lockland for a tasting."

"Pais won't drink, but I bet Vince would like that."

"So. How much would you miss them? If you didn't live seven minutes away from them in Lexington?"

Chantele tipped her head and narrowed her eyes at him.

"Hmm?"

"Like...if you lived...in Rodey. But you could drive there to see them. Instead of living there and driving here to see me?"

Chantele took a deep breath, the idea of living closer to Rye making her smile.

"Where would I live? Like is there something available in Rodey? Or would I have to find something in Kissing Springs? Or Bardstown?"

"There is a place in Rodey," he told her.

"Oh." She nodded. "Okay. Where? Maybe we can go see it this weekend?"

"Chan." Rye kissed her again. "I'm asking you to move in with me."

"You want—? You're—?" She bit her lip, but the sharp bite of her teeth did nothing to hold her happy grin back.

"Yes. We've been seeing each other for six months. Maybe that's not long for some people, but I know."

"You know what?"

"You're the one for me," he said simply.

The last time she had visited, just before Paisley had the baby, Rye had told her he loved her. What had struck her as so romantic was that they were on a picnic when he told her. They'd ridden Rosebud and Fleet out to the far corner of that pasture behind the barn at Pressey's. Rye had led her right to a spot where a picnic had already been prepared for them—complete with ice-cold lemonade, fried chicken, and coleslaw. She'd been in awe of the picture it created—the red and white checked tablecloth, the sun high in the bright blue cloudless sky, and the green that surrounded them.

Later, she had thought to ask him how he'd managed to get it set up when he'd been with her. And she had been floored when he admitted his mom had helped him with it. She'd met his parents, but only a few times, and they'd never been overly affectionate in front of them. But the picnic itself, the fact that his mom had made the fried chicken and the apple pie they had for dessert, had spoken volumes to Chantele about his feelings for her.

So much so that it only felt right, complete, when they sat side-by-side sipping their lemonade and he kissed her cheek and told her he was in love with her.

Despite their inauspicious start, the verbal sparring in the Iron Stag and her disastrous attempt to seduce him by riding that damned bull, once they'd started talking, Chantele couldn't imagine things happening any differently that they had.

"I love you, too," she told him that day on their picnic.

Still, she hadn't expected an invite to move in so soon.

Then again, they were both adults and both ready for the next step, which in retrospect was the biggest reason why the hookup at the Iron Stag had failed.

"What about work?"

"I know you can work from home," he answered. "You've already told me that."

She laughed softly. "But what if I don't want to? What if I quit that job? Found something here?"

"Something in mind?"

"Lots of distilleries in this part of the country."

Rye arched an eyebrow at her. "You want to distill whiskey?"

She snorted. "No, although it could be fun. But I'm assuming distilleries need marketing people. And if not, I can do other things. I'd work in production. That would be great."

Rye rubbed his thumb over her lips. "Do what makes you happy. As long as you do what makes me happy and move in with me."

"You should know I have baby fever," she warned him, a cautious hand on his chest.

"Well, in that case, I have something for you."

Chantele swallowed hard when he moved off the couch and disappeared down the hall. The butterfly storm in her belly kicked up a notch when he returned with a small, wrapped box in his hands.

"Rye?" she whispered.

"Just open it." He pushed it at her gently. Chantele's hands shook as she tore the silver paper off the box. It was flat and square, not a traditional shape for a ring. More like a pair of earrings or maybe a bracelet. Would he have gotten her jewelry? She didn't wear much, so it didn't seem likely that Rye would have taken a guess at what sorts of styles she liked.

She flipped the top of the box off to reveal a small gold padlock.

"Oh my God." She laughed, but her eyes burned with tears. With trembling fingers, she took it from the box and then lifted the keys from under it. Their initials were engraved in the flat body of the lock.

"I want to get you a ring," he said quietly. "But I want you to pick it out."

"Rye." Lock and keys still in her hand, she leaned forward and kissed him. "This is perfect."

"I thought we could lock it on the bridge when your friends come to visit."

"Wow." She laughed. "Really?"

"I mean, we can. Or we could just go do it by ourselves this weekend."

Chantele loved that Rye was sentimental enough to want to do the lock bridge as a symbol of their commitment. She wouldn't blame him at all for not wanting to do that in front of her friends. Hell, she still had a few weekends left to fix breakfast. Although Nova was in the hot seat now. Vince had bet her she couldn't finish a marathon; she might have it if she hadn't pulled a hamstring.

"I don't wanna wait," she decided. She didn't want to wait. The lock might be symbolic but what was an engagement ring if not symbolic of love? Rye's smile in response was all the assurance she needed.

***

Thank you for reading Seducing You. If you enjoyed Chantele & Rye's story, please consider leaving a review on your favorite bookish site.

Keep reading for a sneak peek at Shameless Santa, Welcome to Kissing Springs, Book #7.

SNEAK PEEK AT SHAMELESS SANTA

Chapter 1

November 2021

Stella galloped through the kitchen on her stick horse. Taj Bailey glanced at his little girl as he opened the oven door to check the chicken and noodle casserole he'd popped in for dinner.

"I'm gonna win the race, Daddy," she announced as she circled around at the far wall and hurried back.

"You're not racing anybody, Stella."

Taj clenched his teeth together before he could snap at Ellery. The six-year-old had recently adopted a bossy attitude toward Stella—only four. Taj figured it was probably normal, but it grated on his nerves because Ellery sounded like his ex-wife when she did it. It was inevitable that his daughters would look, talk, and act a little like Marley, but damned if he wanted them to pick up his ex's snippy tone and nagging words.

"She's fine, El," he said quietly. "What're you working on there?"

The spitfire blonde at the table looked up at him with a toothless grin. Ellery was a miniature Marley, from her soft, fine blond hair to her bright blue eyes and lively smile. All the things that had drawn him to Marley in the first place, but he found he liked them a million times better in his daughter.

"A picture for Santa."

Ellery pushed the paper over the table and climbed to sit on her knees so she could study the picture with him. Taj stepped away from the oven and leaned over the table. Standing this close to her, he smelled the grape-flavored soap and lotion his mom had given the girls with their candy buckets for Halloween.

"See, Daddy?" Ellery pointed a long, skinny finger at the picture she'd drawn. "This is Mommy's house. And Santa always comes in the door, cuz we don't have a chimney. And this is Stella." A wave of warmth rushed over him when Ellery moved her finger to a little stick figure with a pink skirt on and a stick horse in hand. Ellery had that part right; Stella seldom went anywhere without Rosie.

"What's this?" He tapped a shape on the page that resembled a van.

"Mommy's van," Ellery answered. "And this is Rebel."

"Where are you in this picture?"

"Here." Ellery moved her finger to a face in an upstairs window.

Taj laughed and went back to the oven. Stella zipped through the room again, this time talking to Rosie as she rode. Taj peeled the foil on the dish back, checked the timer again, and decided it was about ready. He removed the foil altogether and pushed the dish back into the oven for a few more minutes, as per his mom's directions.

"What're you doing in the window, Ellery Boo?"

"Watchin' for Santa!"

"You know Santa doesn't come until you're sleeping."

Ellery shrugged and pulled the paper close to her again. Taj watched her study the pile of crayons on the table and finally choose green and then turned away to get plates and cups to set the table.

"Hey, cowgirl," he called to Stella. "You need to tether your horse. Dinner's ready."

"Not hungry!" Stella sang back as she galloped back by him.

"All cowgirls and boys have to eat, Stella Bean," he said calmly. If Ellery was a mini-Marley, Stella was his little twin. At four, she was solid, short and compact—Taj wasn't short, but he was thick with muscle. He'd started lifting and cardio workouts when he was twelve. Bull-riding and horsemanship called for being fit, although when he was that age, he might have had other reasons to drop the baby fat.

Girls.

Stella heaved an exaggerated sigh as she stepped over the stick to dismount. Taj pressed his lips together to hide the smile. His baby hadn't just inherited his dark hair, eyes, and compact build; she was often broody and in a foul mood, too. He supposed he had himself to blame, always grouchy and frustrated with Marley.

Thank God that was finally over. It felt to him like the divorce lasted longer than his marriage. He and his ex would never be friends, but at least now she was out of his life, other than co-parenting the girls. She even had a new husband, poor sucker, so she didn't need Taj for anything. Which meant he could loosen up and put all of that—except his girls—behind him and be happy and fun again. Hopefully, *that* would rub off on Stella.

"Ellery, time to eat." He put the stack of cups on the table and turned back for silverware.

"Almost done, Daddy!"

Stella climbed up on the bench across from her sister and leaned her elbows on the table.

"That's not what Rebel looks like."

"Is too."

"Daddy, tell ElryBoo Rebel is cute. Not ugly like that."

"Stop it, Stella!" Ellery shouted. Taj glanced over his shoulder as he opened the oven again. Ellery was still bent over her drawing, intent on the finishing touches.

"Stella, be nice," he told his youngest. He grabbed the oven mitts from the counter, took the dish from the oven, and put it on a hot pad.

"Rebel's tail is longer, too," Stella whispered.

"Shut up, Stel!" Ellery yelled.

Taj dished up small servings of his mom's casserole for both girls. They loved chicken and noodles; both girls always claimed the dish as their favorite. He could still see the way Marley's shoulders tensed every time either of the girls said so.

Ellery dropped her crayon, almost like a mic drop, and sat back, eyes on the drawing. Taj put the silverware on the table, amused when he saw that Ellery had signed the drawing like an artist would. He took the milk from the refrigerator and poured an equal amount in two glasses, relieved to see Ellery putting her crayons away.

"Daddy, are you drinking milk, too?" Stella asked him.

"I'm drinking water, Stel," he told her.

"You should drink milk. 's good for your bones. Gramma says so."

"I drank a lot of milk when I was little like you girls."

"I'm a big girl," Ellery corrected him.

"Now I drink milk in the morning."

"With your breakfast?" Stella asked him.

Taj filled a glass with ice water, served himself some of the casserole, and sat down beside Stella. He'd sat by Ellery last night; the girls were strict about things like that. If he didn't follow the rules, one of them got jealous.

"We're posted to pray, Daddy."

"You're right." Taj tousled Stella's dark curls and nodded. "Who's turn?"

"Mine." Ellery's tone brooked no argument.

"Okay."

Taj folded his hands and tipped his chin down as Ellery asked God to bless their food. Thankfully, their dinner prayers were shorter than bedtime prayers. Ellery had the tendency to ask God to bless everyone from Mommy and Daddy to the dental hygienist to the squirrel she saw cross the street and run up the tree on the way home from her first day of school a few months ago.

"This is yummy," Ellery announced after shoveling a bite into her mouth. Taj flinched; the noodles were hot, and Ellery hadn't blown on her fork at all. As he expected, she frowned and covered her mouth.

"Blow on it, Stel," he reminded Stella before she could do the same as her sister. She took a deep breath and blew on the food like the Big Bad Wolf.

"Gil doesn't like capseroles," Ellery told him when she finally dropped her hand and started to chew. "He says they're for po boys."

Taj clacked his molars together and counted to three in his head. Gil Foley was Marley's new husband and unfortunately, the girls' new stepfather. Taj hadn't liked the guy much before Marley married him, but now that Gil had opinions about how his daughters should be raised, Taj couldn't stand the guy.

"Do you think that's true?" he asked when he trusted himself not to sound angry.

"What's a po boy?" Stella asked. She blew on her food again, though Taj figured by now, it was at least room temperature.

"I like Gramma's capseroles," Ellery answered him. Taj nodded and ignored Stella's question. He didn't like to ignore the girls, and he didn't do it often. But Gil and anything he said was a sore subject, and he didn't want to talk about the man in front of his girls.

"What did you add to your picture, El?" He scooped his own bite of the hot noodle and chicken casserole and stuck it in his mouth. When his fork was clean, he pointed it at the paper Ellery had pushed to the side of the table.

"A cat."

Taj reached for the paper and drew it closer so he could see it better. "Why did you add a cat?"

"Because Gil said we could have one. I want Santa to bring me one."

"You can have the cat," Stella mumbled. Taj fought the urge to high five the girl. There were times when the girls brought Rebel over. He didn't mind. In fact, he'd wanted Rebel in the divorce, just like he wanted the girls. Marley flat out refused to let him take the dog; at least he got partial custody of the girls.

He damned sure had no plans to let them bring a cat over here.

"What's that?" Taj pointed his fork at a rectangle in front of the house. It was red and white with something unintelligible scribbled on it.

"For sales sign." Ellery rolled her eyes at him as if the answer was obvious.

"For sale sign?" Taj frowned. "What for sale sign?"

"The one Mommy and Gil put there."

"Where are Mommy and Gil going?"

"We're gonna live with Santa!" Stella squealed.

Too much dread in his stomach now to eat, Taj pushed his plate away and looked at Stella. She stared him down with his own dark eyes, but a playful grin tugged at her little mouth.

"Santa?" he repeated. What the hell had Marley and Gil been telling the girls? Were they telling them they were going to the North Pole?

"Yeah. In Californ-i-a."

Taj shifted his attention back to Ellery, who drew the word out and pronounced the I and A with long vowel sounds.

"California?" He sounded dumb, and he had the presence of mind to be glad Gil wasn't here to watch him stutter. On the other hand, this was something he and Marley should discuss, whatever the hell it was the girls were telling him.

"Yep. Santa Rosa." Ellery nodded and scooped up another bite. "I was scared to move, because I was afraid Santa wouldn't know where to find me and Stella Bean. But when Mommy said Santa Rosa, I knew it would be okay."

Taj blinked silently at his oldest daughter.

Santa Rosa.

Santa Rosa, California?

And this news was coming from his six-year-old daughter rather than his ex-wife?

"I'm asking Santa for a new horse," Stella told Ellery.

"Rosie's not a real horse." Ellery rolled her eyes with disdain, and visions of Marley flashed in Taj's mind again.

"Santa will bring me a real horse," Stella informed her sister.

They were kids. What would a six and a four-year-old know about their mom's plans to move across country? Taj took a deep breath and reminded himself to stay calm. He would mention it to Marley tomorrow when he took the girls back to her.

But he had a feeling this was real. Why else would Ellery have included the damned for sale sign in her drawing if it wasn't already stuck in Marley's front yard?

Want to keep reading and find out more about Taj Bailey? Click here:

Shameless Santa

Shameless Santa, Welcome to Kissing Springs, Book #6

Sunshine & Soulmates, Kissing Springs The Sunshine Season, Book #12

Bourbon & Bedposts, Kissing Springs The Bourbon Season, Book #18

ALSO BY TRACY BROEMMER

Women's Fiction Novels:

Luther's Cross (10th Anniversary Edition)

Fairytale (Writing as Therese Kinkaide)

Just Like Them

Small Hours

Picket Fences

Two Story Home

Green-Eyed Girl

Say Everything

Come Home for Christmas

Sketching Litchfield Lake

Ever, Again

Safe as Houses

Damsel

The Valentine Suite

Women's Fiction Series in Order

Lorelei Bluffs

Every Little Thing

Two A.M.

Blind

Leaving July

Hesitation Marks

Four Letter Words

See Kate

Loved You More

A Lorelei Ending

I Do

The Williams Legacy

Truth Is

Other People's Ugly

Omissions

Women's Fiction Short Stories

India Falls

Luther's Cross: 87,600

The Candy Cane Tree of Willow Lane

Delays

Same Time Next Year

Contemporary Romance Novels

Destiny's Calling: Your Future is Waiting

Wedding Day Shenanigans

Holiday Fling

The Kiss Off

Something Like Love

Plus One

End in Flames

Contemporary Romance Series In Order

The Mississippi Queen Trilogy

Love, Nashville

Forever, Duncan

Always, Jess

Truly, Dante (A Short Story)

The H Books

Gettin' Hitched

Hookin' Up'

Holdin' On (A Novella)

Timberton Hounds (Novellas)

Priceless Memory (A Short Story)

Endless Summer

Homeless Holiday

Restless Hearts (Currently included in Fall Into Love, an anthology by Fluffy Fox Publishing)

515 Whiskey

Intoxicate Me (A Novella)

Taste Me

Kissing Springs Trio

Shameless Santa

Sunshine & Soulmates

Bourbon & Bedposts

Lockland Distilling: Keys to Love Trilogy & Kissing Springs World

Leaving You (A Short Story)

Seducing You (A Novella)

Kissing You (A Novella—currently included in the Let's Get Naughty, Volume 2)

Shared World Novels

Hold Onto the Stars (Blue Collar Romance Series, Book #5)

The Jane Thing (Meet Cute Book Club Series, Book #2)

Shameless Santa (Welcome to Kissing Springs, Book #7)

Doctor Divine (Doctors of Eastport, Season 2)

Sunshine & Soulmates (Welcome to Kissing Springs, Book #

Bourbon & Bedposts (Welcome to Kissing Springs, Book #

Moonlight in Montreal (The Vagabond Series)

Beach Daze (Flamingo Island)

Christmas & Other Inconveniences (Betting on Christmas Collection)

Love in Motion Duet (Novellas)

Feels on Wheels

Rings on Wings

The Wine Tasting Series (Short Romantic Stories)

Perfect Pictures (Traminette)

Coming Home (Edelweiss)

Save Me Every Dance (Rosé)

Marry Me (Shiraz)

Birthday Wishes (Muscat)

Dad Jeans (Vignoles)

Contemporary Romance Novellas

Boone's Girl

Today, Again

Indian Summer

Dear Jaclyn Perris

Mistletoe Mishaps

Deadman's Hollow

French Stuff

Holdin' On

Toasted

End in Flames

Endless Summer

Homeless Holiday

Feels on Wheels

Rings on Wings

Intoxicate Me

Contemporary Romance Short Stories

Truest Love (Currently included in Show of Dreams anthology)

Swipe for Fangs (Currently included in the anthology Welcome to Whynot)

Mrs. Bennett

Peppermint Lane

The Principles of Accounting

Strawberry Wine

Love Letter

Sambuca Santa

Truly Dante

Leaving You

Priceless Memory

Perfect Pictures (Traminette)

Coming Home (Edelweiss)

Save Me Every Dance (Rosé)

Marry Me (Shiraz)

Birthday Wishes (Muscat)

Dad Jeans (Vignoles)

Other Novellas

The Devy Man, A Horror Novella

The Keeper's Heart, A Horror Novella

Anthologies

Just Coffee — French Stuff (2020)

Snowed Inn, Vol. 1 — Holdin' On (2020)

Aced, Back to School — Boone's Girl (2021)

Snowed Inn, Vol. 2 — Delays (2021)

Sweet Treats — Peppermint Lane (2021)

Sweet Sprinkles — Same Time Next Year (2022)

Rescue Me — End in Flames (2022)

•

Fall Into Love — Feels on Wheels (2022)

Cool Off — Endless Summer (2022)

Fall Back Into Love — Rings on Wings (2022)

Backing the Bluegrass — Leaving You (2022)

Kissing Santa Claus — Sambuca Santa (2022)

Let's Get Naughty — Homeless Holiday (2022)

XOXO — Trusting Cupid (2023)

Mrs. Right — Mrs. Bennett (2023)

Tease Me — Taste Me (2023)

Falling for the Boss — The Principles of Accounting (2023)

Ride a Cowboy — Seducing You (2023)

Love and Coffee — Makin' Whoopsie! (2023)

Fall Into Love — Restless Hearts (2023)

Welcome to Whynot — Swipe for Fangs (2023)

Let's Get Naughty, Volume 2 — Kissing You (2023)

Show of Dreams — Truest Love

ABOUT THE AUTHOR

Tracy Broemmer is the author of several contemporary romance novels including The H Books, Wedding Day Shenanigans, and the Mississippi Queen Trilogy. Tracy also writes women's fiction and is the author of the Williams Legacy series as well as several stand-alone titles.

Tracy's books have been called gripping, emotional, and timely, and readers describe her characters as real and relatable.

Tracy lives in Midwestern Illinois with her husband of 30 years. Visit her on the web and sign up for her newsletter at www.broemmerbooks.com

www.ingramcontent.com/pod-product-compliance
Lightning Source LLC
Chambersburg PA
CBHW020248130626
46549CB00005B/2126
9781951637712